HARLEQUIN®
Presents

Enjoy eight new titles from Harlequin Presents in August!

Lucy Monroe brings you her next story in the fabulous ROYAL BRIDES series, and look out for Carole Mortimer's second seductive Sicilian in her trilogy THE SICILIANS. Don't miss Miranda Lee's ruthless millionaire, Sarah Morgan's gorgeous Greek tycoon, Trish Morey's Italian boss and Jennie Lucas's forced bride! Plus, be sure to read Kate Hardy's story of passion leading to pregnancy in *One Night, One Baby,* and the fantastic *Taken by the Maverick Millionaire* by Anna Cleary!

We'd love to hear what you think about Presents. E-mail us at Presents@hmb.co.uk or join in the discussions at www.iheartpre̶s̶e̶n̶t̶s̶ and www.sensationalroman̶c̶e̶ where you'll also find ̶ ̶ ̶ books and authors̶

D07359l5

Even if work is rather boring at times, there is one person making the office a whole lot more interesting: the boss!

Dark and dangerous, alpha and powerful, rich and ruthless… He's in control, he knows what he wants and he's going to get it! He's tall, handsome, breathtakingly attractive. And there's one outcome that's never in doubt: the heroines of these sparky, supersexy stories will be

From sensible suits...into satin sheets!

A brand-new miniseries only available from Harlequin Presents!

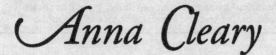

Anna Cleary

TAKEN BY THE
MAVERICK MILLIONAIRE

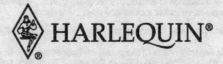

Undressed
BY THE BOSS

HARLEQUIN®

TORONTO • NEW YORK • LONDON
AMSTERDAM • PARIS • SYDNEY • HAMBURG
STOCKHOLM • ATHENS • TOKYO • MILAN • MADRID
PRAGUE • WARSAW • BUDAPEST • AUCKLAND

ISBN-13: 978-0-373-12754-2
ISBN-10:   0-373-12754-5

TAKEN BY THE MAVERICK MILLIONAIRE

First North American Publication 2008.

All about the author...
Anna Cleary

As a child, **ANNA CLEARY** loved reading so much that during the midnight hours she was forced to read with a torch under the bedcovers to lull the suspicions of her sleep-obsessed parents. From an early age, she dreamed of writing her own books. She saw herself in a stone cottage by the sea, wearing a velvet smoking jacket and sipping sherry, like Somerset Maugham.

In real life she became a schoolteacher, during which her greatest pleasure was teaching children to write beautiful stories.

A little while ago, she and one of her friends made a pact to each write the first chapter of a romance novel over their holidays. From writing her very first line, Anna was hooked, and she gave up teaching to become a full-time writer. She now lives in Queensland with a deeply sensitive and intelligent cat. She prefers champagne to sherry, and loves music, books, four-legged creatures, trees, movies and restaurants.

For Beth, the heroine of my heart.

PROLOGUE

TOM RUSSELL stood BY his father's grave and surveyed the rolling pastures. The morning was fresh with smells of earth and grass. All the way to the boundary fence the grass sprang tall, its lush green enriched by its contrast with the flat brown stubble of the farmer's on the other side. His private creek, fed by the mighty Hunter, was awash, little waterfalls gurgling down its pebbly path, the willows on its bank glowing with new greenery, soaking their privileged toes.

Horse country. Heartland of the Russell newspaper dynasty. And now it was his.

If he could hang onto it.

He drew the crumpled paper from his jeans pocket and smoothed it out. Though he knew them by heart, the spidery words sprang out to gut him afresh.

> My son,
> By now you'll know what I've done. I want you to understand, boy, that I did it for you as much as for charity. Sometimes a man needs a shock to see what's important. The big money's gone, but you're a true newspaperman at heart, like your old man, and you can probably save Russell Inc if you want to.
> Tom, I lost a woman once myself, and I know what it is to grieve. But I also know that the best way to get over

a woman is to find another one. You've still got your shares in the company and a little bit of property. Find yourself a nice girl who doesn't care about money…

As always when he reached that line, Tom crushed the letter in his fist and shoved it back into his pocket. The irony of it.

Another woman.

That was always his father's solution.

As if there could be a woman to replace Sandra. But he could rebuild his inheritance. He could use what was left to claw it all back. In the meantime, he could trade on his reputation and his finance skills to keep what was left of the corporation ticking over. Marry it off to the highest bidder, if necessary. Keep the cash flowing, pay the salaries… Pay the bequests to his stepsisters.

It could be done. It *could*.

If he could keep his father's last act a secret. All he needed were weeks. Just a few more weeks…

CHAPTER ONE

MARCUS RUSSELL was dead. Tom, his brilliant, ruthless son, had taken charge of his empire. On the Friday morning of the memorial service, two weeks after the old media magnate had been buried under a Hunter Valley gum tree, cathedral bells rang out across Sydney Harbour, summoning the rich and powerful to pay their respects.

In the dressing room of his hotel suite, Tom Russell gave his reflection a critical last glance. His charcoal suit was cut with the required elegance, enhancing the athletic power of his well-made frame. Likewise, his ebony shirt of finest Italian fabric, his pearl silk tie and hand-stitched shoes. If his blood pressure was slightly elevated, the tense little beat in his temple was contained. His steel-grey eyes held the usual degree of sardonic assurance, his harsh, tanned face the control.

No one would guess the nightmare he was living.

He held out his hands and accorded them grim approval. Steady as a rock.

With his raven hair cut crisp and close, he was as groomed, sleek and polished as any of the race of high-flying billionaires he belonged to. *Used* to belong to. And would again.

He clenched his lean hands. If—*if* he could keep the lid on.

* * *

From her desk at the *Sydney Clarion*'s newsroom, Cate Summerfield could see the Russell yacht, its flags at half-mast, embarked on a graceful honour lap of Sydney Harbour.

'Just look at that,' Cate glowered, narrowing her green eyes. 'It's probably worth enough to feed Africa for a decade.'

The schooner bowed to the swell, its white sails billowing against the glittering blue. It had been reported that Tom Russell had outfitted the luxury vessel into a floating hospital, so the waves could lull his dying father to sleep on the days he could find no rest.

It was a far cry from the care Cate could afford for her darling gran. The frail souls at the Autumn Leaves Nursing Home counted themselves lucky even to have beds to rest their aching old bones in. The nurses didn't even have time to feed the helpless ones. Patients like Gran, who was on the waiting list for heart surgery, had to rely on their relatives to come in and help them eat their evening meals. It was probably that cold reality that had spurred Cate to be unusually terse in the obituary she'd written for the media mogul.

She'd done thorough research, digging through the archives of all the rival news chains—Russell's own, even the powerful Wests. Conscientious in her attempts to achieve balance, she hadn't shrunk from quoting some of his harshest critics, including a choice selection of the epithets his enemies had used to flay him. The piece was her best so far, in her modest opinion. Honest, she'd judged it, though Marge on the neighbouring desk had called it *'biting.'*

She'd held her breath after she'd filed it, but it had made it past the legal hawks and gone to press. Afterwards people in the newsroom seemed to look at her differently. Steve Wilson, the *Clarion*'s star reporter and resident heartbreaker, had stopped referring to her as Blondie for at least a day, and Harry, their Chief of Staff, whom she'd never seen show any emotion in two years, had raised his eyebrows and whistled.

Still, even a work of art wouldn't win her a spot on the front page. That would go to the journalist lucky enough to cover the memorial service.

Cate turned her gaze to the newsroom. Though early, already above the ceaseless background buzz of the television monitors the room was alive with the tapping of keyboards, and the constant ringing of the phones.

'The sharks are circling.' Marge winked towards a little cluster of glory chasers gathered around the news desk.

The news journalists were lounging about, swapping languid yarns, but everyone knew what they were after. They were waiting for Harry to announce whom he'd chosen to represent the *Clarion* at the memorial, salivating for the chance to corner Tom Russell.

Cate's money was on Steve, who boasted more contacts than Telstra. Even though she'd been engaged to him for a stressful forty-seven days, and knew how clever he was, to her mind Barbara, whose lovely face and sleek hair accompanied a razor-sharp brain, or tough, experienced Toni, who chewed politicians for breakfast, were equally deserving. They all had a special sort of gloss that had nothing to do with conditioning treatments.

She sighed and pushed a long, wavy strand of her pale hair back behind one ear.

If—*when*—she joined that elite group, she'd write stories that mattered. She'd build up a readership, renegotiate her salary. Make it big with a few stories, earn some respect…

Cate grimaced. Dream on, girl. The *Clarion* was renowned for its fearless battle against corruption in high places. It had taken down many a politician or dishonest businessman, but she couldn't take personal credit for any of them. In her two years there, she'd worked on everything except the columns that counted.

On the night their engagement had crashed, among other vicious remarks Steve Wilson had made about what he called her obsessive concern for Gran, he'd sneered that she was too soft to make a top news reporter. Even Marge said she tried too hard to think the best of people.

They couldn't be more wrong. Underneath Cate's annoying curls, pale skin and the soft curves bequeathed to her by some Scandinavian ancestor, she was tougher than she looked. Long before Gran's heart emergency, she'd been dying to rip open the fat underbelly of the privileged rich and expose them with her brave, incisive words.

All she needed was a chance to report on someone living. Dead people, even dead media legends, didn't generate scoops. Scoops went with live players. And if she was ever to get off Obituaries, a scoop was what she had to have.

She leafed back through her photo file to a rare shot she'd unearthed of Tom Russell. Now, he was alive. At thirty-four, his harsh, sardonic face with his glinting grey eyes, arrogant cheekbones and firm, masculine chin, was stirring in its vitality.

'Did you manage to dig any dirt on him?' Marge said, peering over at the image, her lively brown eyes alight with interest.

Cate hesitated. She'd dug up heaps on old Marcus. It had been easy.

As a young woman, Gran had worked for one of his big dailies, before he'd sacked her and some of her colleagues in order to turn his respected newspaper into a trashy tabloid. Everything he'd done since had only reinforced Gran's anger with him.

Gran had never missed an opportunity to point out the evils of his ways. Even in Cate's eyes he'd done nothing of value with his wealth, except to indulge his own extravagant tastes and flamboyant lifestyle.

His son, though, was a more elusive target. Tom Russell had spent a number of years in England, running the Russell media enterprises there. Gran had never had much to say about him.

'I only found what everyone knows,' she said, handing Marge the photo. 'You know, about how he came back here to take over a few years ago when the old man first took ill.

The ruthless strategic war he's waging against Olivia West's chain—'

'Not to mention the ruthless strategic war he's waging against us.'

Cate shrugged. 'Well, he is a businessman. It's strange, though. I couldn't find a thing about his private life, except the tragedy, of course. Nothing at all about girlfriends.'

The truth was that, since the death of Tom Russell's wife in a car accident in England a couple of years ago, very little of a personal nature was ever reported about him. He was never seen at the big society bashes or charity dos.

'His wife was somebody famous, wasn't she? Wasn't she a scientist?'

Marge nodded. 'Medical research. Some genetic studies, I think.'

'Well, she doesn't sound like the usual trophy wife men like him seem to go for. Are you sure there would be dirt?' Cate met Marge's cheerful, cynical gaze. 'Maybe Tom isn't over her death.'

'Oh,' Marge scoffed, 'give me a break. She died two years ago, but I'm sure I heard they were separated long before that. Anyway, a man like him knows how to move on. You can't be that rich without being a villain, one way or another. He's a man. And a very attractive one.' She gave the photo a tap. 'Think of the world he's been brought up in. He'd have women by the boatload.' She frowned at Cate. 'Now, don't you start going soft on him. I thought you said you'd given up being sucked in by heartless machos.'

'I have.' Cate's gaze was uncontrollably drawn towards the vicinity of the desk. She was over Steve. She really was. It was hard to believe she'd ever had to creep to the ladies' room to cry when he'd flaunted his girlfriends at the Friday after-work pub session, though, humiliatingly, on the rare occasions she was now able to join them, everyone still looked at her to see how she was taking it.

'I definitely am,' she assured Marge. 'But you still have to give people the benefit of the doubt. Just because Tom looks like that…and has that unfortunate background…'

Unmoved by the counsel for the defence, Marge shook her head. 'Sorry. It doesn't look good for him.'

Cate frowned. At twenty-five she was hardly naïve, especially after her brief, soul-destroying plunge into lunacy with Steve, and she had to acknowledge the likelihood of Marge's words. Tom Russell had been brought up by a father whose endless stream of actresses and models must have caused serious pain for his succession of wives.

She studied the photo. Was he as callous as Gran had so often described his old man? Those cool grey eyes roused an unquiet little buzz in her insides. Her gaze shifted to his mouth. A lot could be deduced from a man's mouth. His had been chiselled in severe lines and was wide and firm, the upper lip straight, the lower one very slightly fuller. There was no softness there, though more than a suggestion of irony. He didn't need to spike up his hair to make himself look taller.

She turned the photo sideways. Sexy, from all angles.

'Cate.'

She started. It took a second for it to filter through to her that Harry had come out of his huddle with the news editor, and seemed to be looking her way.

Her? He wanted *her*?

She pushed her chair back and rose to stroll the length of the newsroom, vaguely conscious of Steve's, Toni's and Barbara's startled gazes whipping around to stare.

At the desk the others looked up to watch and listen while Harry's sharp eyes appraised her from beneath his bushy brows.

'Your Russell obit wasn't all that bad,' he stated.

She gazed at Harry through a mystified fog. Were there bells ringing somewhere? Then pleasure, sharp and furious, streamed through her to her toes. 'Oh. Oh, thank you. Thanks, Chief. Thanks very much,' she stammered, feeling her ears turn pink.

She continued to babble her thanks, but Harry ignored her.

'See what you can make of the memorial,' he instructed with laconic calm. 'The business people, the politicians who've been invited, who's in and who's out—the tone of it. Above all, watch Tom Russell. Who he talks to, who his friends are. Take Mike with you. They're not allowing cameras inside the cathedral, but get there early and see who you can catch on the red carpet. There's a lunch in some undisclosed location. Press are excluded.'

She nodded. A huge, joyous whoop had risen inside her and threatened to burst out, but Harry wasn't the sort to encourage a hug, so she squashed it down.

'Oh, and, Cate—security will be tight. Don't forget your pass. And don't even think of trying to get to Russell. He's a dangerous man to cross.'

She nodded with appropriate newsroom nonchalance, and turned to stroll back to her desk. The little cluster of ace reporters fell back silently to allow her through. She permitted herself one glance at Steve Wilson. He was frowning hard, his ginger spikes quivering, his blue eyes narrowed. Pity it made him look slightly cross-eyed. She should have noticed that sooner.

Everything—the day, the sunshine streaming in through the window, the newsroom—felt suddenly fantastic, as if it was her day. She grabbed some notebooks, pencils and her miniature tape recorder and stuffed them into her handbag. Then she paused a moment to glance down at her dress, beginning to show signs of washing stress. Not quite the thing for a society memorial.

Black. She needed something black.

A vintage suit she'd bought from Rhapsodie, the boutique down the road from her Kirribilli boarding house, was itching for a new outing. She glanced at her watch. Nearly eight thirty. The service was slated for noon and she and Mike, her photographer, would need to set up at least two hours earlier. Time enough to catch the train home.

She found Mike in the canteen, poring over the racing page. She had a hurried conference with him, and a bare thirty minutes later was running up the stairs of the Lady Musgrave.

Her eighties suit was a stunning fit. The slim skirt fell to just above her knees, while the jacket had big, sewn-in shoulder pads and a severely shaped bodice with a modest, though deep-cut neckline. Extremely flattering to her breasts, although hanging the press pass around her neck rather ruined the effect. She tried clamping the pass to her jacket hem, considered it with a frown, then took it off to worry about later.

The other nineteen occupants she shared the boarding house with had left for work, so she had the bathroom to herself. In the presence of black, her blonde hair had turned to a pleasing silvery ash. With no time to waste, she subdued the mass by tying it in her nape with a black velvet ribbon. Black heels and pearl earrings completed the effect.

Not too much later, dressed to kill in vintage Carla Zampatti, she found Mike at the rear of the cathedral with his camera, leaning his long, lanky bones against a brick wall.

Streets had been cordoned off to control traffic, and the cathedral precinct was quiet, apart from a battalion of security guards prowling the boundaries, mobiles to their ears, and an occasional black-clad cleric hurrying across the grounds. There were a couple of big, expensive cars in the visitors' car park, but no other sign yet of the rich and famous.

A team of television journalists arrived to set up in the front. Cate exchanged mobile codes with Mike, and went to reconnoitre the cathedral.

A security guard with a shaven head was stationed in the porch. She showed him her press ID, and after a growled warning not to even *dream* of trying to use her mobile inside if she didn't want it confiscated, he consulted a list before allowing her to pass. She grinned to herself. Fat chance they had of enforcing that rule.

A reception table had been set inside the door, and she

helped herself to a programme, which included a sketchy seating plan. As she'd expected, the pews allocated to the press were at the rear.

The cathedral's soaring interior was cool and dim. At once the deep hush washed over her, reminding her it was some time since she'd been in a church. Awed by the graceful lines of the architecture, she strolled about, examining the stained glass and reading wall inscriptions.

Two women carrying magnificent flower arrangements bustled in from the transept aisle. Cate paused, drinking in the atmosphere. Even the presence of a couple of security guards lurking behind pillars, keeping a watchful eye on her in case she broke into some anti-Russell guerilla activity, couldn't dilute the spiritual repose of the place.

A priest attending to something in the chancel looked hard at her as if he knew a red-hot sinner when he saw one, and, shamed, she slipped into a pew. She sent up a small prayer for her grandmother. Perhaps heaven wanted vengeance for the damage she'd caused Gran, because a small nagging need she'd been vaguely conscious of for some time suddenly became compelling.

The priest finished his preparations and hurried away. Cate gazed after him. Down that aisle, she knew, were the vestry and church offices. There had to be a ladies' room. Should she risk it, though? She wasn't sure the general public were allowed into the inner reaches of the cathedral.

The sound of voices alerted her to the arrival of more guests. She noticed that the security men were both scanning the people crowding the entrance. Taking advantage of the distraction, she rose to her feet. It was now or never.

Hoping she looked like a woman with nothing to hide, she walked coolly down towards the altar, asserting her feminine right to visit the ladies in her dignified gait. No one intercepted her, and when she made a quick turn into the transept aisle, and saw a long, wide hallway stretching ahead, she was grateful to see it devoid of either security or clergy. With her heart hammering at the strange guilt attached to stealing around a church like a thief, she hastened past a couple of unmarked doors, not daring to open them for fear of surprising someone, and turned into the vestry.

A maze of rooms opened from it. There was one with a piano, a robing room lined with alcoves hung with priestly vestments, and a business office adjacent to a small meeting room. In the office the computer was running, as though someone had recently stood up from it and taken a temporary break.

She hesitated, feeling more like a trespasser with every step, then spotted a promising door on the other side of the meeting room. To her relief, it belonged to a tiny washroom, with a small washbasin below a rust-flecked mirror, and a toilet cubicle redolent of disinfectant. To her grateful eyes it looked like heaven.

Afterwards, when she'd washed her hands and tidied some wisps straying from her silvery mane, she opened the door, prepared to exit, then froze. There was movement in the meeting room.

Instinctively she pushed the toilet door to, not quite closing it for fear of alerting the security guard, priest, or whoever, of her presence, while she summoned enough nerve to sashay forth with careless aplomb.

She strained her ears. Had she imagined the sound? Almost at once then the clack of a woman's heels approached and came to a halt somewhere alarmingly close by.

She nearly dropped dead with fright when a rather throaty, feminine, cigarette-husky voice said, 'Oh, Tom. Commiserations about your dad. I'm so terribly sorry. I know exactly what you're going through.'

There was a curt, masculine murmur of response.

Cate closed her eyes and prayed that Tom Russell was not the man outside the door about to discover her breaching his costly security arrangements.

'And as if it wasn't enough losing your father, without some of the rubbish being printed about him. Did you see that disgusting obituary in the *Clarion*?'

Cate stopped breathing.

'I saw it.'

Though the tone was grim, the deep voice had a dark, liquid quality. Like liquid velvet. Dark, dark brown velvet. Black, even.

'Where do those jackals get the nerve?' the female voice went on. 'All that hogwash about editorial independence. Will you sue?'

Cate's heart jumped into her throat, then Tom Russell said, 'Wouldn't they love that? I hope I have more subtlety. Don't worry, I'll deal with Miss What's-her-name. In *my* way.'

A chill shivered down Cate's spine. In *his* way. What was his way?

He spoke again. 'Eventually they'll all work for me. For *us*. Won't they, Livvie?' Cate pricked up her ears, then felt ashamed. She was acting like a voyeur. What she should do now was to walk out there, excuse herself, and make a swift, dignified exit. And she would. Just as soon as she screwed up the courage.

Her heart thundered so loudly she felt sure they must hear it, for the woman's voice issued through with perfect clarity.

'That's why I need to talk to you. It's about our deal.' There was urgency in the woman's tone.

'This isn't a good moment, Liv. As you might be able to imagine, I have things on my mind today.' The response was polite, but Cate detected a sardonic tinge to it.

'Well, how about this afternoon? After the lunch?'

'Impossible. I have urgent meetings scheduled that can't be postponed.'

'Nothing is more urgent than *this*,' the woman hissed. 'Listen to me, Tom. Everything's at risk. Malcolm has heard something. He's playing every card he can to hold up the divorce. Somehow he's got wind of the merger, so he's asking for a much bigger slice of the company.' She paused, then added, 'My grandfather didn't build an empire for it to end up being controlled by the likes of him.' There was a hoarse vehemence to the contralto voice.

Cate's ears rang with the possibilities. She had a sudden inkling into the woman's identity. Surely that voice was familiar. With her heart thumping, and careful to make no sound, she moved to the door and risked putting her eye to the crack.

Her gaze lighted on a portion of long leg encased in some dark, expensive fabric, brushing a highly polished black masculine shoe. Next to the shoe rested an elegant black briefcase. Then the man moved further into her view, and her heart lurched in her chest.

It was Tom Russell all right, in the living flesh, negligently leaning his tall frame against an ornately carved piece of church furniture. Though his hands were shoved carelessly into his trouser pockets, there was a coiled tension about him. His black eyebrows were lowered over his cool grey eyes as he scoured his female companion with an alert, intelligent gaze.

Forget what Marge had said about him being attractive. He was so hot he *sizzled*.

Cate moved her head, trying to see the woman, but she only caught a rear-view glimpse of gleaming copper hair confined at the nape in a sophisticated black snood. It was enough though, she thought with wild excitement. The next words, as abrasive as sandpaper in Tom Russell's stern, accusing voice, confirmed her suspicion.

'I thought you understood how crucial secrecy is at this stage, Olivia. Bloody hell, what sort of a businesswoman are you?'

Olivia. The woman was Olivia *West*.

Cate's brain buzzed into overdrive. She was onto the scoop of the century. What her editor would give to know this. Russell's joining with the West Corporation. It would be the merger of the tabloid Titans. This was more than mere front page stuff. This meant headlines.

She had to get out of there and write it. In a sudden brilliant inspiration, she shoved her hand into her bag and connected with the minuscule cassette recorder Gran had given her. Her heart skipped an excited beat. Here was a golden opportunity. She'd be the toast of the newsroom. What reporter could resist? Although—Harry was pretty firm on the ethics of recording people without their knowledge. Her fingers hovered over the button while she waged a war with her conscience. Regretfully, the thought of Harry's flinty gaze, and his strictures about the journalism code won.

At the same time as the powerful redhead's response floated through to her she realised, with a sinking feeling, it was too late to announce her presence. Already, she knew too much.

She surrendered to the inevitable and put her eye to the crack again, in time to catch a glimpse of Tom Russell prowling about with his lithe, long-legged stride.

And he was worth watching. Though he seemed tense, it was clear that underneath the sombre black shirt, the pearl grey silk tie, the Armani—the suit could be nothing less—his lean, long bones, muscle and sinew were all working together in a veritable symphony of co-ordination.

Unfazed by his critical tone, Olivia West was launched into a feisty come-back. 'It could just as easily have been someone from *your* side who leaked. Anyway, Malcolm doesn't really know anything for certain, he's just guessing with that diabolical genius he has for ferreting things out about people. He only wants to hurt me. I need your help with this.'

Tom Russell shot back, 'I never let domestic arrangements interfere with business. Yours are hardly my concern.'

'But this does concern you,' Olivia West retorted. 'Look at it this way. I won't go on with our merger until I'm free and clear of Malcolm. And if he manages to hold up the court process for three or more months—and he can if the court believes his claim is worth investigating—our deal will collapse. You know it must.'

Every line of Tom Russell's big, lean frame was charged with impatience. 'Well, for pity's sake, make a deal. Give him enough of what he asks for to make him feel he's scored something.'

'I've given him enough,' Olivia said fiercely. 'I've given him everything. He's *taken* everything. He's not getting any more of my company. But that's not even the reason he's doing this. It's not about the money. It's about *you*.'

Tom Russell came to a sudden halt, right in Cate's line of vision.

She stayed glued to the sight, until Olivia West spun in to obstruct the view. Despite the media baroness's artful make-up, her face was strained. Her glossy red lips were compressed and she held her hands, gloved in slinky black lace, clasped in front of her voluptuous chest.

Cate frowned. Was that much cleavage strictly appropriate for a church service?

Olivia turned her back, spoiling Cate's view of her. 'Look,' she said, 'I'm sure you know Malcolm has always been insanely jealous of you. Some fool's informed him of the times we've met to negotiate, and he's had the ridiculous idea that you and I are—together. Perhaps even contemplating marriage.'

Tom Russell stood very still, then said, his voice dangerously soft, 'Now, how could he possibly get an idea like that?'

Olivia must have felt the sudden scary escalation in the tension, because she attempted to lighten it with a husky laugh. 'Well, it's not so outrageous, is it? We're both attractive people, both high achievers, our backgrounds are similar, we have things in common… Everyone knows how perfect you and Sandra were together. But you've been without a wife a long time, Tom. Sooner or later…' The unmistakable purr in her voice made Cate squirm with discomfort. Was Olivia testing the water in hopes of seducing Tom Russell? *Marrying* him?

'My wife is dead.' The rebuke hung on the air, as stinging as a face slap.

Cate caught her breath in the charged little silence that followed. Tom Russell's feelings for his wife must still be very raw. Still, she felt a wave of sympathy for Olivia. If he'd spoken like that to her she'd have cringed.

But the glamorous redhead was made of tougher stuff, because she managed a careless laugh. What a remarkable woman, Cate marvelled. To possess such self-control. How fabulous to be able to maintain her poise after such a forbidding rejection.

'Well, there's no need to look so stern, Thomas. I'm only reporting what Malcolm has dreamed up in his fevered brain. And because he believes it, he's looking for ways to hurt us by holding up the divorce.' She added, her voice as soft, distinct, and every bit as steely as Tom Russell's, 'And until my divorce goes through, darling, there will be no merger. And you and I will *both* lose a lot of money.'

'Then you must advise him of the truth very quickly, Livvie.' The icy chill permeated the store-room door with bluetooth penetration.

'He's not likely to believe what I tell him, is he? Look, the answer's simple enough. All you need to do is to show him you have another woman.'

Tom Russell gave an incredulous laugh. 'What other woman?'

'Now, now, Tom.' Sly amusement stole into the low voice. 'Don't try to tell me you can't come up with a woman—like *that*.'

Tom Russell surveyed her grimly. 'I think you've been reading your own tabloids, Olivia. Forget it.'

'For goodness' sake, can't you follow in your old dad's footsteps for a week or two and find some nubile little actress to flash around the town? It's only for a few weeks.'

'I'm not my old dad,' Tom Russell said, his voice ominously soft.

There was a small, tense silence, then Olivia West snapped,

'*Think* about it.' She crossed into Cate's view, stepping up to Tom and boldly placing her hands on his shoulders. In her chic black dress, her curvaceous figure looked formidably seductive. 'We both have a lot to lose, don't we, darling? How much do you want your merger?'

With implacable calm Tom Russell detached her and pushed her away. 'Not enough to deceive some woman. For God's sake, I'm a businessman, not some tabloid Don Juan.'

'That's not what I mean,' Olivia exploded hoarsely, swinging away from him. '*Hire* a woman. You only need to let Malcolm see you with her a couple of times. Once I get my divorce, you'll have your merger. And I'm not deceiving Malcolm. For your information it was *he* who—' Her voice grew strident with emotion. 'Look, in a few minutes time this church will be packed with people, and a good number of them will be actresses who work for your television network. Some of them, I'm willing to bet, have already been employed in more ways than one by your old dad. Pick one of them. Offer her money.'

Cate nearly gasped out loud at the audacity of the woman. How would Tom Russell take such a crack about his father? She strained to hear, but the abrupt click of a door closing suggested that Olivia had delivered her parting shot, and stalked off.

Cate sagged with relief. Thank heavens. Now Tom would follow, and she could creep from her hiding place and hightail it back to Mike.

There was the sound of a chair scraping, and the room fell quiet. She moved to the opening in the door to check that the coast was clear, and came up short. To her intense annoyance Tom Russell was still there at the table, frowning over some papers.

Damn the man. She fretted with impatience. People would have started to arrive by now and she'd be missing her chances. She exhaled a frustrated breath, then took a harder look at him. In his unconsciousness of being under scrutiny, the lines in the tanned skin around his eyes and mouth suddenly seemed more deeply etched, as though from tiredness or strain. She felt a stir of sympathy. Perhaps even a Tom Russell could spend sleepless nights grieving. The loss of a parent was no small thing, as she could testify.

She sighed, and, bracing for a wait, closed her eyes and leaned back against the sink.

A shrill jangling broke out at her feet and she nearly jumped out of her skin.

It was her mobile phone.

She stood paralysed for helpless seconds while the ghastly tune went on. Then adrenaline rushed to her rescue and she was overcome by a false, fatalistic calm. She plunged her nerveless hand into her bag, brought the phone up and held it to her ear.

'All right, Mike,' she said. Her soft voice crashed into the charged silence. 'I won't be long.'

She did the only thing possible. She put the phone away, and, her limbs stiff with embarrassment, jerked the door open and walked out of the ladies' room, straight into the big, iron-hard frame of Tom Russell.

CHAPTER TWO

TOM'S first impression was of softness. Soft breasts pressed against his chest, soft, firm thighs, a delicious feminine fragrance rising from a tender white neck.

He felt the woman gasp and try to recoil, but his hands swiftly gripped her upper arms. She trembled in his grasp, her white satin flesh alive with a sensual vibrance that instantly communicated itself to him.

His gaze clashed with large sea-green eyes, sparkling up into his in alarmed calculation. Her rosy mouth was full, ripe and passionate. Some crazed part of his brain actually considered the possibility of sinking his teeth into her plump lower lip.

Common sense told him this was no mere blonde. Ridiculous words like 'spy' and 'industrial espionage' jostled in his brain. Her parted lips made a tiny, anxious tremor and he felt a grim, cynical triumph.

Well might she be anxious. Stirred against his will, he demanded harshly, 'What the bloody hell are you doing in here?'

Cate's brain blurred into sensory overload. Steel-grey eyes, glittering with suspicion, scoured her face. She had a dizzy awareness of the faint, clean scents of soap and sandalwood, of fine, expensive fabrics brushing her skin. But underneath those outer trappings of masculine sophistication her feminine sensors picked up the heady, high-voltage buzz of pure essence of *man*.

For whole seconds her lungs forgot to work, until she forced some action. 'I was just—I was—' She took a deep breath and said in a more assertive voice, though it might have skipped into a slightly higher register, 'Would you let me go, please?'

He tightened his grip for an instant, as if to demonstrate how completely he had her in his power, then abruptly released her. While she made an emphatic point of rubbing her arms, he whipped a wafer-thin phone from inside the jacket of his superbly tailored charcoal suit.

'Explain yourself while I call Security,' he commanded, flicking it open. He perused the dial, no mercy in the set of his chiselled mouth and jaw. She grappled with a million excuses, but one clash with the icy blaze of his grey eyes through their black lashes told her all of them would fail.

The vision of herself being escorted from the cathedral between beefy security men, in the glare of a thousand cameras, was unthinkable. How would she explain to Harry? She'd be the laughing stock of the newsroom.

She lifted her chin, and prepared to surrender the truth.

'I was—visiting the Ladies,' she said with an attempt at airiness, though she could feel a slight flush colour her cheeks. Privately, it was mortifying. Of all the people in the world to have to explain to…

His eyes made a slow, thorough, entirely masculine survey of her down to her ankles, then back, lingering an insolent moment on her mouth. 'Do you seriously expect me to believe that?'

She stared at him in incredulity. 'Well…' A saving surge of anger brought the words flying to her tongue. 'Why shouldn't you believe it? People are innocent until proven guilty in this country, you know.' She drew herself up to her full five-six. 'And now I have to go. There are things I need to do.' She made a brusque attempt to sweep past him, but his lean bronzed hand shot out and closed once more around her arm.

'Not so fast.' He moved very close to her, and again she

felt that swamping effect on her senses. 'Don't try to play the innocent, Goldilocks. You've been lurking in there like a common thief, spying on a private conversation. Either explain yourself properly, or you will find yourself in court pretty bloody quick.'

There was something so insulting about being called a name in that deep, cultured voice. Allowances needed to be made, she supposed, for a man coping with the loss of his father, but did he have to be so offensive? Certainly, neither her shoes nor her suit were brand new, but they were far from common.

'I wasn't listening to your conversation.' In a determined effort she twisted from his grasp and retreated a strategic step. 'I had important things on my mind.'

He snarled a contemptuous expletive not at all appropriate for a church, and added, 'Don't make the mistake of assuming you're dealing with a fool, darling.'

The air fairly crackled with masculine aggression. Who knew what he might do? For all she knew, he might have minders who rubbed people out, like the mob.

To get herself off the hook, she warmed to her innocence theme, ignoring his sceptical gaze raking her from head to toe as if she were some despicable form of alien low-life. Amazing how, in the living, breathing flesh, that stern, tightly compressed mouth could still be so sensuous and expressive.

'I hardly heard a thing,' she continued, earnest in her effort to allay his fears. 'You can't hear much at all in that room when the door's closed.'

'Rubbish. I heard *your* voice very, very distinctly.'

She rolled her eyes. 'Look, I was here first, remember? I didn't know you were coming in for your romantic rendez-vous, did I? I'm not a mind-reader. I came in to find the Ladies, and you chose to use this room, too. Maybe I should have let you know I was there, but I thought you and your— girlfriend would be less embarrassed if I just said nothing and tiptoed away.'

He took a moment to digest this, and his gaze became less hostile, though more guarded, as if he'd seen the force of her argument but didn't want to show it. It occurred to her that underneath his big, powerful, macho-male-in-command act, he actually seemed quite worried. She wondered if the merger had a lot more riding on it than he'd been willing to show Olivia West.

His eyes flickered over her. 'What's your name?'

Her heart sank. Lying was tempting, especially considering her summation of Marcus Russell as a vampire whose fangs had been battened to the national throat, but she thought of the guard in the porch and discarded it. 'It's Cate,' she muttered. She forced herself to meet his eyes. 'Summerfield.'

'Summerfield.' His brow creased, as if with the effort of recollection, and he slipped the phone back into his pocket.

That little action reminded her of something that had been nagging at her. He hadn't made the call to Security. No minders had been summoned. Why?

The answer came to her in a dazzling flash. Because it would be a risk. Of course!

He was afraid that if he did, she would blab his secret to the world.

For a fabulous, golden moment she tasted the heady nectar of power. How the tables were turned. Goldilocks held Tom Russell in the palm of her little hand. Just wait—*wait* until he found out where she worked.

He'd relaxed a little, and now he started strolling about, pausing at times to fire questions and grill her with his hard gaze, although she couldn't help noticing now how often his eyes lighted on her legs, or drifted to her hair.

Her own blood sparked up in response. She reminded herself that he was a rich, spoiled parasite devising criminal new ways to soak up the country's wealth, but even at his iciest, his tall, dark sexiness impacted on her with undeniable power.

'So who are you?' he shot at her in his deep voice. 'Are

you an actress? A friend of one of my stepsisters? What do you do? More to the point, why are you here?'

She fluttered her lashes. 'Oh, that.' She allowed the moment to lengthen, the better to savour it.

Though a cowardly part of her cringed in terror at the risk she was about to take, another part fairly tingled with anticipation. She could feel his wolfish grey eyes follow her every move, and somehow the knowledge incited in her a dangerous desire to tease him.

With pleasurable deliberation, she pulled the ribbon from her hair, shook out the pale mass until it frothed in a blonde cascade down her back, then smoothed it all down with her hands.

Against every fibre of his will, Tom's concentration wavered as the line of her profile and tender white neck impinged on his vision. His brain, locked down and blinkered against temptresses since the solemn vows of his wedding, flooded with images of shapely mermaids and bare ripe breasts. The thought came to him that she should be sunning herself on some rock. Naked, and smelling of the sea.

Conscious of his riveted attention, Cate swathed her hair back into her nape, casting him a glance as she retied the ribbon. 'You invited me.' She made a graceful, self-correcting gesture. 'That is to say—my employer was invited to send a representative.'

'Your employer…' His thick black brows edged together and he flicked a frowning look over her. Then she saw the grim comprehension dawn in his eyes. He slapped his forehead with the palm of his hand. 'Bloody hell. I should have realised. You've got paparazzi written all over you.' Underneath the derision, she detected something very close to dismay in his voice.

In one heart-stopping stride he was across the room to where she stood. 'Here, give me that.' He snatched the bag from her shoulder, and her alarmed internal organs all dropped back into their niches. 'Which rag do you write for?' he growled, making a ruthless search of the compartments. He found her phone and coolly slid it into his jacket pocket, then his lip curled in triumph as he pounced on her cassette recorder.

'No, I don't work for you,' she rejoined, watching with some pleasure as his lean, smooth fingers rewound the tape and played it back without finding a whisper of illegal conversation. 'I'm not guilty of churning out any of that cheap Russell trash, thank you. I write for a quality paper. The *Clarion*.'

He gave a snort of cynical laughter. 'Quality? The *Clarion*?' He put the recorder back in her purse and took out her pass. 'What's your excuse for not wearing this? I'd sack you for that alone if you worked for me.'

'It spoiled the line of my jacket.'

'What?' His lip curled with such incredulous contempt that she was spurred to anger herself. A man like him would never know the challenges a woman faced fitting in with the society crowd.

He thrust the bag back at her. 'Let me impress on you, Miss Summerfield,' he said, enunciating each syllable with punishing precision, 'anything you *did* happen to hear is completely off the record. Don't even think of trying to use it.' He towered over her in such an intimidating stance that it took all her nerve to hold his gaze. 'Though you did say, didn't you,' he added, his eyes narrowing, 'you didn't hear anything?' He scoured her face. 'How true is that?'

Maybe it was the excess of testosterone in the air, but somehow her feminine spirit seemed creatively inspired.

'Nearly true,' she assured him, hoisting her bag to her shoulder. She gazed at him with smiling innocence. 'Unless you count that bit about the merger. But don't you worry. I don't know much at all about share prices and the Stock Exchange.'

It was like kerosene to the bonfire. He hissed in a long searing breath, and stood stock still. Then he began to advance on her, his grey eyes glinting through the screen of his black lashes. 'What else?' he murmured, his deep, rich voice smooth with menace. 'What else did you hear?'

Her heart revved up to an insane degree, but there was a crazy exhilaration in taunting him that drove her on. She gave a breezy little shrug and neatly eluded his grasp, sashaying over to the table to take a look at his notes.

'Nothing else,' she threw over her shoulder. 'Oh, except the part about Ms West's divorce. Something about deceiving the courts so she can rip off her husband in the division of property, et cetera. It was all really too complicated for me to take in.' She shuffled through the pages and slanted him a mocking glance. 'And then there was that bit about how you have to hire a woman.' She gave an amused laugh.

He stared at her for seconds, his eyes narrowed in calculation, then strolled across and tweaked the pages from her grasp. In a visible change of tack, he perched casually on the edge of the table, quite close to where she stood.

Too close for comfort.

'Now, how does a female body,' he drawled, cool amusement in his deep, dark voice as he made a slow, appreciative appraisal of her from head to toe, 'so clearly designed for an angel, come to house such a teasing little devil?'

In spite of herself her blood heat rose. She told herself she was impervious to flattery. Her body wasn't like an angel's, unless it was a fallen angel that had consumed one chocolate too many. She made an effort to keep her voice under control. 'I'm—just doing my job.'

'Now, now, Cate.' His mouth edged up in a smile. It gleamed in his grey gaze and lit his harsh, sardonic face with such warmth, it was impossible to believe she'd not seen at once how handsome he was. 'You know you can't write a word of it. Think of your code of ethics. Wasn't it the *Clarion* who invented it?'

He was all suave reason and charm. She knew he was turning on the seduction, but it worked. All the air was sucked from her lungs and her heart started an erratic thumping.

'The code, yes,' she agreed, breathless. 'We do, we do—

adhere to it. Religiously. Although if something's in the national interest—I'm sure Harry would think that a merger between Russell's and the West Corporation—'

'Won't happen if you publish it.' He still smiled, but the warmth vanished. 'Olivia will pull out. Then I'll sue you for a billion and take your *Clarion* to the cleaners.'

The cold menace in the words helped her to pull herself together. She fished in her bag for a notebook. 'That sounds like a threat, Mr Russell.' She challenged him with her eyes. 'Hang on, I'll just write it down.'

Danger flashed in his grey irises like a lightning strike. 'Take care, sweetheart. This is not the day to be playing games with someone who can ruin you.' He gestured at her accusingly. 'Consider your position. Here you are, *caught red-handed*, listening in on a conversation in which some highly sensitive information is being discussed. You've deliberately concealed your press pass—'

She gave a deep sigh. 'I explained that.' Resigning herself, she capitulated, feeling in her bag for the pass, then lifting up the edge of her jacket while she clamped it on. 'See? Ruins it.'

His eyes were fastened to her waist. He must have only seen the merest fragment of bare skin over her ribs before she dropped the hem back, but his pupils dilated and she saw his heavy black lashes give an almost imperceptible flicker. He raised his darkened gaze to hers.

Somehow she couldn't look away. The air tautened and she felt her mouth dry. She pulled the pass off and patted down the hem several unneccessary times, conscious of her heart's sudden mad racketing.

A priest's dark figure loomed in the doorway, and they both started. A gang of small, fresh-faced boys crowding in behind him told her that the choir had arrived. She became fully conscious then of something she'd had at the edge of her awareness for some time, but had been too intensely absorbed in Tom Russell to notice.

The organ was playing, and there was a growing swell of voices.

The church was filling up.

'I'd—I'd better go,' she said, making an abrupt move towards the door, looking for a way through the milling boys. 'I don't want to miss my spot in the church.'

'No, you don't.' Tom Russell sprang to his feet and caught her elbow. 'I'm not letting you out of my sight.'

Visions of Mike, outside, fuming, assailed her. 'But—I have to do my job—'

His hand closed around her wrist in a deceptively light grip. 'Until I decide what to do with you, sweetheart,' he said softly, 'you're with me.'

CHAPTER THREE

IT FELT surreal, walking into the main chapel with Tom Russell. All over the church heads swivelled their way, and there was an added buzz to the murmurs of the congregation. Everywhere she looked, she met the interested stares of celebrities and socialites, business high-fliers and politicians, plenty of whom had tasted dust, courtesy of the *Sydney Clarion*.

She had the unnerving sensation that she was in the maw of the enemy. A small crowd surged to greet Tom, but she couldn't help noticing that, despite their sombre murmurs of sympathy, their curious glances kept shifting sideways to scrutinise *her*.

Perhaps their interest mightn't have been as avid if he hadn't been keeping such a firm hold on her arm. A stylish older woman, who looked vaguely familiar, rushed up to engulf him in an emotional embrace and he was forced to relax his grip. Cate saw her opportunity, and tried to slip away, only to feel a ruthless hand grasp hers and draw her back. Despite her sudden shock, or because of it, his hard palm in sudden connection with hers sent her blood coursing in giddy confusion.

The woman appeared to be one of Marcus Russell's ex-wives. 'Who's your friend, Thomas?' she demanded, leaning forward to peer closely at Cate once her effusions had run out. 'Introduce me.'

Tom Russell's caustic gaze clashed with Cate's. 'No one you want to know.'

The woman looked taken aback, then, when his attention was diverted by the next well-wisher, whispered to Cate, 'Don't take any notice of him, dear. This is a difficult day for him.'

Of course. It must be, Cate thought with some remorse. How could she have taken such pleasure in taunting him?

The service was surprisingly simple and austere. Though the chapel was packed to the rafters with celebrities, there was none of the razzmatazz Sydney had come to associate with Marcus Russell. Someone had chosen the most exquisite, spiritually moving music in the repertoire. If music could waft Marcus's poor old soul to heaven, Cate reflected, then J. S. Bach and Mozart's 'Requiem' should do it.

She gave up trying to escape to Mike, and allowed herself to be jammed into the front pew beside Tom Russell and a gaggle of expensively dressed stepsisters and their mothers, who all stared at her with surprise and curiosity. Some of the glances at her suit made her wonder if she'd left the price tag showing. She crossed her ankles under the seat, hoping to spare her shoes from their merciless scrutiny. She prayed when the others prayed, and sang the Twenty-third Psalm along with everyone else.

A stream of dignitaries, including the Prime Minister, stood up to honour the memory of Marcus Russell, but after a tedious while she tuned down to listen with half an ear, and started to plan her story for tomorrow's issue. Her absent, wandering gaze drifted down to the burnished leather shoe resting next to hers, and she surfaced from her reverie with a small start of surprise. Why hadn't she noticed before?

Between Tom Russell's trouser hem and his expensive loafer was an expanse of bare, tanned skin.

He'd forgotten his socks.

A strange sensation flooded her, of sympathy and amusement mingled with some poignant, melty feeling. How unex-

pectedly human it made him. She was overwhelmed with a
need to turn and look at him, to touch one of the beautiful lean
hands resting on his Armani-clad knee. Possible words of
comfort welled up on her tongue, but she forced herself to
keep gazing straight ahead, and had to be satisfied with
drinking in the magnetism of his masculine aura, and luxuri-
ating in the warm contact of his arm and shoulder.

When he rose to take the lectern, the coughs and shuffles
of the congregation ceased, and the church fell silent. The air
pulsed with anticipation. She held her breath for him, wondering how nervous he was.

If he was it didn't show. Like a man born to rule, he rose
to the occasion and spoke with dignity and authority, taking
only an occasional glance at his notes. His voice resonated
through the church like the darker tones of a cello.

It gave her a perfect opportunity to study the classic bone
structure of his lean, harsh face. He was so tall and master-
ful, so sincere and grief-stricken and restrained, she felt
moved. How he must have loved that dreadful old man.

It came as a shock. Affection for his only child was the one
thing she'd never heard Marcus Russell accused of. She knew
a stab of discomfort to wonder how much the unshrinking
honesty of her obituary had added to Tom's pain.

'My father may not have been universally admired,' he said,
controlling the emotion in his voice, 'but he was a generous
benefactor to many charities. Those who knew him well knew
that he was *not* "a mere leech, fat on the profits of greed".'

The familiar words, read with grim distaste, jolted through
Cate. Murmurs of sympathetic outrage rippled around the
congregation.

She sank down in her seat. What if they knew the perpe-
trator of those words was here in their very midst?

From his commanding position at the lectern, Tom spoke
to the sea of familiar faces before him without seeing a single
one. Conscious this had to be the performance of his life, he

measured his comments with care, searingly conscious of their irony. If people only guessed how generous his father had been to charity.

The question that had tortured fourteen sleepless nights tormented him afresh. Why had Marcus done it? How could a man of his experience have believed a desperate financial shortfall would change his son's life for the better? Did he really believe a disaster could erase a man's grief?

Something of the depths of his dismay must have leaked into his voice, because the hushed atmosphere suddenly seemed charged with dynamite.

'In fact,' he read on, frowning in the effort to concentrate on the task at hand, 'far from "squandering his squalid profits on sordid pleasure", throughout his life my father was a notable phil—'

A sudden connection pinged in his brain and with a little choke he broke off. The notes blurred, while in his mind's eye, in perfect clarity, a name focused.

Cate Summerfield.

The people, the church, the rigorously composed thread of his address receded. He raised his eyes from the page.

Cate Summerfield, *obituary* writer, stared back at him from her pew, frozen in guilty acknowledgement. Her mermaid's eyes were wide in alarm, her lips tight-pressed.

In the throbbing silence, the emotional tension ratcheted up to screeching pitch and sobs broke out, but Tom was hardly aware of them. For speechless seconds he grappled with the sheer enormity of it. The nerve of this dizzy little blonde to have shown her face, even to have set foot in the church. But to have eavesdropped on a negotiation that gave her the actual power to ruin him…

For a heart-struck instant he stared into an abyss. If the corporation went under thousands would lose their livelihoods. The Russell name would echo down the years as a byword of shame.

Conscious of a faint, unwonted moisture on his upper lip,

he had to grip the lectern tight to restrain himself from loosening his collar. But he wasn't his father's son for nothing. With an almost superhuman effort, he summoned his formidable powers of recovery and cut the unnecessary emotion to make a lightning situation assessment.

Damage control needed to be neat and complete. He must find something to offer her. Some way to zip her saucy mouth with its infuriating smile. He thought of a bribe and discarded it. How the *Clarion* would gloat. Although if there was something she wanted, something out of her reach…

What could he offer her? The answer boomeranged back at once. What else would she want, but what they all did? She was a reporter, after all.

Beyond that, he seethed, she was a woman. And in that crystalline instant he knew exactly how he could do it.

Cowering in her pew, Cate recognised sudden purpose in Tom Russell's glinting gaze. She gathered herself to make a dash for the exit, but too late, for with an eloquent gesture that provoked a wave of sobs around the cathedral, he handed over the lectern to the officiating archbishop, and in a couple of strides was back beside her.

'Stay put,' he hissed in her ear, smiling, though his white, even teeth were gritted. 'I'm not finished with you yet.' He slipped his arm around her and held her close against his hard body, as though she were some stricken family member in need of support. Her senses plunged into uproar, but she shrank from making a scene, and submitted to the disturbing effects of feeling his long muscled thigh pressed against hers.

In a short, nerve-racking while the service came to an end, and she knew her time had come. As soon as the mourners rose to make their way out, her captor seized the opportunity, amid the confusion, to hustle her away from the goggling stares of his family members, down the aisle past the crowded vestry, and out through the door to the visitor's car park.

As they emerged into the sunshine a long, low black limousine, its darkened windows blank and sinister, drew up along-side them. Visions assailed Cate of being strangled and dumped on some highway.

'Get in,' he said, opening the rear door. And when she hesitated to dive into what looked impossibly like some sultan's cave, complete with oriental rugs, sumptuous cushioned seats and silken panelling—'*Please.*' In the sunlight his cool grey eyes glittered inscrutably against his tan. 'We need to talk. I have a proposition for you.'

Please on his brusque tongue was unexpected enough to be reassuring. After a moment she bowed her head in acquiescence, climbed in and slid as best she could to the far side of the deeply cushioned divan-seat. With a few curt instructions to the driver, Tom Russell joined her, and closed the glass barrier.

His elegantly clad knee was only centimetres from hers. She moistened her lips, overly conscious of his high-octane masculinity in the opulent space. She crossed her legs, then uncrossed them when she saw his gaze flicker down to them.

'Alone at last,' he drawled.

'I had no idea limos were furnished like this,' she said nervously.

'This was my father's car.' His lip curled. 'His most recent mistress had a taste for the exotic.'

To her alarm the engine purred into life and the car moved towards the street-exit. 'I thought you said you just wanted us to talk?'

'Aren't we talking?' He lounged back to survey her with a considering gaze, his black lashes half lowered.

She wished she didn't have to be so aware of him, and tried not to notice the relaxed idleness of his long limbs and smooth, tanned hands. 'Shouldn't you be with your guests now? I mean, as they—as they leave the church, don't you want to be there in the front porch to shake hands with everyone?'

'No, I don't.'

They'd left the cathedral yard and were now weaving their way through traffic. Where to? she thought with panic. Some execution site?

She took the risk of meeting his sardonic gaze. 'But isn't there some sort of a—gathering or something? I mean, don't you have refreshments, or a luncheon party, or—or—' The limo took a turn towards the eastern suburbs. She struggled to think of some compelling reason for them to turn back. 'Don't you have things you want to say to your guests,' she tried in desperation, 'to thank them? You know, for their concern, and their good wishes?'

A tinge of amusement crossed his face. 'Those self-indulgent sink-holes of the nation's wealth? No, I'm more interested in the things I want to say to you. But now you remind me...' He pressed something in the pleated silk wall and a door slid open, revealing an elegant little cabinet containing decanters and glasses. He selected a crystal balloon glass and poured a drop into it of pure liquid amber. 'Cognac?'

To be honest, she wasn't very good with alcohol. It had a tendency to go straight to her head. But when was the last time she'd been in a travelling pasha's den with a billionaire? She accepted the balloon with as casual a nod as if she drank the stuff every day of the week, and stole a glance into its depths. Fire glowed in it, and it seemed to be alive with a strange, electric beauty. She inhaled, and the intoxicating aroma rose to fill her head.

She risked a tiny sip. It melted into her lips, and suffused her mouth and throat with a seductive, tingling warmth that irradiated her entire being like the rays of the sun on a winter's morn.

Her eyes watered with the effort of trying not to cough, but she still had to, anyway.

He waited for her to recover, an amused quirk disturbing the stern line of his chiselled mouth. 'I want to make a deal with you.'

'What sort of a deal?' Though warmed by the cognac, she

reminded herself to be cautious. She said hoarsely, 'I hope you know nothing will tempt me to compromise my journalistic standards.'

He broke into a laugh. It lit his eyes and made them crinkle up at the corners. 'What standards?' Then he caught her glance and his face grew solemn. 'I would never try to tempt you from your standards, Cate. But I can give you something you want, and you can give me something I need.'

'Really? What's that?' The cognac, or maybe his deep laugh, had melted into her bloodstream and infused her voice with a husky quality she could have done without.

He made a gesture with one bronzed hand. 'You want your story. I'm prepared to give it to you. First break, even ahead of my own newspapers. Full disclosure of the merger. Interview—photographs—everything.'

Excitement surged to her head. Full disclosure would give her a far more meaningful scoop than a few lines that were light on details, but heavy on hints and guesses. And an actual interview with him! It would take her right up there with Steve and Barbara. She could get Gran into a private hospital and…

She roused herself from her fantasies, and caught him studying her face. His eyes were veiled, but his sexy mouth had edged into a very slight smile, like a wolf with a tasty little goose in its sights. It stirred her misgivings. 'What's the catch?'

'Ah, the catch.' He straightened up a little, as if to gain more leverage in the contest. 'The catch is that you must wait for three weeks to publish. If you can't promise that, I'll spill the story this afternoon and the merger will collapse.' He gave her a moment to digest, his eyes intent on her face, then added softly, 'And then you'll have nothing to report.'

She frowned. Three weeks was an eternity in publishing. Could she trust him to keep his word? A man with his cool, uncompromising mouth was unlikely to be a slimy liar like

Steve. And if she took into account his stunning eyes and that appealing little cleft in his chin—

She fought down a warm tidal surge in her blood. Really, she must not focus on his physical attributes. She had to remember he was a shark in the ocean of world affairs, and she needed to keep her head. An unnerving thought struck her. The one thing he *did* have going for him was the genuine affection with which he'd talked about his father.

What if he was setting her up to take some sort of revenge for her cutting obituary?

She gave the cognac a wary sip. 'You must realise that I have to report on the memorial today. You're not asking me to falsify the truth, are you?'

A muscle tightened in his jaw. 'I'm asking you to do the *ethical* thing and limit your report to strictly what was on the record. When my merger goes through you can write what you like.'

He was lounging back on the seat, his long limbs lazily disposed, but despite his casual posture she sensed a waiting stillness in him, as though a lot hung on her acceptance. Again she wondered just how important this merger was to Russell Inc. Was the corporate giant in trouble?

Sad creature that she was, she considered drawing out his suspense, taking her time to agree so as to postpone the moment when he dropped her from the enchanted limo and she plummeted back into ordinary life. A man with such a low opinion of her integrity deserved to be tortured a little.

She sighed. Lucky for him she was cursed with a conscience.

'Oh, all right,' she said, leaning back against the cushions.

She could feel his smouldering gaze scorch her from her hair all the way down to her toes. It was flattering to command such a furnace-blast of attention.

'As well,' he added in an offhand tone, 'today you act as my girlfriend. '

'What?' She sat bolt upright. Shocked at first into a laugh, she stared at him then for incredulous seconds. 'Are you serious? Do you think anyone would believe that? I know my friends would be amazed, not to mention the newsroom. I mean—don't get me wrong, but anyone who knows me knows that you're absolutely the last person on earth I'd ever dream of—'

She broke off in time to realise his lean, harsh face had stiffened. 'I'm relieved to hear it,' he said drily, 'since the feeling is mutual. In fact, your total unsuitability is one of your greatest assets. People will expect me to dump you in five minutes, and I will.'

'Oh.' She cast him a glance through her lashes. It was a revelation to discover that a tall, dark sexy super-supremo could be so sensitive. But with his temper, it seemed prudent to humour him a little. 'Well, if I agreed, what exactly would you expect me to do?'

He shrugged, and gave his cognac a bored swirl. 'Just walk into the luncheon with me. Hang around. Act—like a girlfriend.' He sounded so offhand, it hardly seemed like much of a request. 'You aren't committed to anyone, are you?' His eyes fell on her ringless hands.

Committed. Deep down inside her something lurched. Even after more than a year words like that could still throw her.

It was hard to fall from prospective bride straight back into bright, chirpy single. Perhaps because she still saw Steve at work. She knew, though, it probably wasn't fair to blame him altogether. A young man like him—of course he'd been daunted. He came from a big family and had no concept of how close she and Gran were. Then when Gran had changed overnight from her clever, funny and invincible self and turned into a frail elderly lady, he'd been jealous of the time Cate had had to spend with her.

As always she tried to thrust away thoughts of the scene with Steve the night Gran had been admitted to hospital for tests. His casual words across the hospital bed, devastating for her, near fatal for Gran.

Her own whispered responses, so defensive and emotional.

Gran had been out of it, so they'd thought, but not far enough out.

Her mind shied away from the choking guilt and fear she'd felt when Gran had clutched at her hand and gone into seizure. Why, oh, *why* hadn't she put an end to the scene at once? She should never have allowed Steve anywhere near Gran.

He'd apologised later. Grovelled, in fact. Promised the earth if she'd take him back. Even Gran had urged her to relent. But she never would. A strong, instinctive part of her had known that if a man truly loved a woman, he cared for the people she loved.

She clenched her cognac glass. She'd learned from the love experience. A man expected a woman to devote herself exclusively to him. Give up her own interests. Spend all her weekends at the football, or her evenings watching sport on television, or playing pool with his beer-swilling friends. Until Gran had had her heart bypass and was safe and well, there could be no new love for Cate Summerfield, even if she did ever want to chance that stony road again.

'*Well?*'

Tom Russell's voice roused her, his black brows bristling with impatience.

'No, no,' she assured him. 'Not—currently.'

What was she hiding? Tom wondered, scanning her face with a cynical gaze. 'You don't sound very sure.'

'Of course I'm sure,' she snapped.

'Ah. Then you'll do it.' He raised his glass to his lips and his lashes flickered down.

Cate eyed the determined line of his handsome jaw, and wondered how many people in his life had ever given him opposition.

She wrinkled her brow. 'I suppose I could do it, so long as it doesn't get out. I'm not sure how my grandmother or the people at work would take it.'

There was a second of stunned silence, then he gave a sharp little laugh. 'Are you saying you'd be ashamed to—be with me?'

'Not ashamed, exactly.' His face was picture of bemusement, and she felt some remorse. Naturally he saw himself as a highly desirable property. With people like Olivia West throwing themselves at him from all directions, it was only to be expected. 'It's not *you*, so much as—' She made a vague gesture and mumbled, 'You know. What you represent.'

Struggling to find his way through shifting mists of unreality, Tom scoured her face for signs of teasing. But her big sea-green eyes held only earnestness, and, goddammit, he realised with a deep inner shock, something that looked like pity. When had he, Tom Russell, ever inspired pity?

He stared at her for long seconds with narrowed eyes. 'Then we'd better make sure your family and friends never find out. I would hate to embarrass you.'

Cate bit her lip, aware of having been less than tactful. 'It's not just a case of embarrassment. It's whether my friends would believe I could be seduced—even temporarily by your—' she waved her glass '—your wealth, and all that. And that brings me to—something else I need to get straight.' She took another swallow to bolster her courage, and her voice deepened. 'I hope you mean this purely as a business arrangement, and you're not hoping to whizz me off afterwards to some sleazy downtown hotel room.'

A muscle twitched in his lean, smooth-shaven cheek, and his eyes glittered with a dangerous intensity. After a second he said, 'I'm asking you because, rightly or wrongly, you were on the spot, and I may as well make the most of a bloody annoying situation. As for whether I could seduce you with my wealth...or that I might be planning some afternoon...' He shook his head while he wrestled with the disgraceful concept. Then he tossed off the rest of his cognac and gazed at her with derisive amusement. 'I need someone to act the part. And that's all you'll be required to do, sweet-heart. *Act*.'

'Well, if you're sure. So long as it's only acting. And as long as you honour your part of the deal and don't leak the story without me.'

He hissed in an incredulous breath. 'For some reason,' he exclaimed when he could find the words, 'the people I do business with believe they can trust my word.'

She arched her brows. 'Maybe they're birds of a similar feather.'

Tom experienced a further shock. What did she think he was—some shoddy used-car salesman? What had he ever done to this woman to earn such distrust? A blistering retort rose to his tongue, but he managed to control it, realising it was far more likely to be the things his father was reputed to have done.

'Look,' he said, with an attempt at smoothness, 'we'll just have to trust each other, won't we? I'll be trusting *you* to act convincingly enough to persuade Devlin—'

'Is that Olivia's husband?'

'That's correct—Malcolm Devlin—that we're together. Do you think you can do it?'

Cate sank back into the plush luxury. Could she? It would be a huge risk, a leap into the unknown, but it would give her a fabulous inside view of a society party. She might even get a feature article out of it, once the embargo was lifted. Although…

She let her gaze flicker over his lean, tall sexiness. She would need to take care. He was so damnably attractive, he might talk her into anything.

She gave a shrug. 'I suppose I could give it a go. '

His eyes gleamed. 'So…' He held out an imperious hand. 'Do we have a deal?'

Too late she realised that touching him was a mistake. It was like putting her hand in the fire. His lean, strong hand closed around hers and sparked that blood-stirring electric frisson along her arm she'd thought never to know again, while at the exact same instant some fiery turbulence disturbed the cool grey surface of his irises.

Oh, God. Her insides plunged into chaos. She withdrew her singed hand with what she hoped looked like some sort of poise, and turned to the window in a confused pretence of looking out, her face and neck swamped with heat while her heart galloped for the finish of the Sydney marathon. All at once her black suit felt stifling.

They'd been winding their way through some swank residential streets lined with trees in spring blossom, when the limo took a sudden turn down towards the harbour foreshore. The marina at Rushcutters Bay hoved into view, home to the big, glossy cruisers belonging to the wealthiest of the Sydney yachting set.

They turned off to draw up before the entrance of a white building perched on the edge of the water. The undisclosed location, she realised. With extreme misgivings she viewed the insignia over its entrance—'The Cruising Yacht Club of Australia'.

Not the usual haunt of her social circle. What had she let herself in for?

The driver, a huge burly man with enormous hands who looked like a nightclub bouncer, climbed out, opened her door and stood to attention.

With her throat suddenly dry, she turned to Tom. 'Shouldn't we discuss the logistics of this?'

'What's to discuss?'

'Well…' She clung to the seat, unwilling to leave the comparative safety of the car.

'Go on, go on,' he chivvied. 'Don't keep poor Timmins waiting.'

She swallowed, and murmuring an apology to the massive Timmins, stepped out, to stand unarmed and defenceless before gang headquarters of the *Clarion*'s sworn enemies.

CHAPTER FOUR

TOM RUSSELL got out of the car, slung a brisk arm about Cate's shoulders and urged her towards the glass entrance doors. 'Let's get this over with.'

'But…' She tried to hang back, but he swept her inexorably forward. 'Shouldn't we work out what we're going to say? Shouldn't we get our story straight? Like how we met, and all that?'

He raised his brows. 'You aren't feeling nervous, are you, Cate?'

'Don't be silly.' She made her voice far firmer than she felt. 'Why would I be nervous?'

'Relax.' There was a grim twist to his mouth. 'There'll be no need to tell anyone anything. One look at you will be enough.'

The doors slid open, and as she moved forwards into the foyer she felt his fingers at the nape of her neck. With a quick tug he slipped off her hair ribbon.

'What are you doing?' she cried, reaching to retrieve it. But she was too late. The full mass of her hair tumbled over her shoulders and down her back. Tom Russell slipped the ribbon into his pocket and surveyed her, satisfaction in his gaze.

'There, that's better. Now try not to talk. In fact, it would be a good idea if you avoid my stepsisters and their mothers. And for God's sake don't tell anyone you're a reporter. If anyone tries to question you, move away from them.'

'But I'm sure you'll want me to at least greet your family members. Otherwise, won't it seem rude?'

His frown darkened. 'We're not here for any bloody garden party.'

Behind the reception desk on the other side of the foyer hung a large framed picture of towering waves poised to crash down on a team of grinning sailors leaning backwards off the edge of a yacht. It made Cate seasick just to look at them.

She was orienting herself to the place when Olivia West bustled in from somewhere in the interior of the building. Olivia stopped short when she saw them, her glance flicking from one to the other. A curious expression stole over her face.

'Oh, Tom.' After a moment she moved forward, and greeted Tom as if for the first time that day with an extravagant buffing of cheeks.

'Well, well. What do you know?' she muttered with a little sideways glance at Cate. She looked quickly about the foyer, then her eyes lit on a door to the left of the reception desk. She strode over and peered in. 'Good. Come in here where we can talk. We want to use this room,' she bawled to the receptionist, who seemed nonplussed, possibly wondering why he was being shouted at at such close range.

Frowning, Tom Russell glanced at his watch, then with an impatient gesture followed Olivia into the room. Cate hesitated a moment too long and the door closed in her face, to be opened again almost immediately. Tom motioned her inside with a testy growl, 'Come on, come on.'

The room was a small, light office, lined with glass cases filled with trophies, and more pictures of intrepid yachtsmen cresting dangerous seas.

Olivia stalked to centre floor and whirled about to give Cate a hard, cold stare. She tilted a sardonic eyebrow at Tom. 'I see you wasted no time. Nothing could surprise me about what a man is capable of, but, I must admit, even *I'm* left breathless.'

Tom introduced them, but although Olivia's greeting was polite enough, her examination of Cate was super-critical.

'Yes, yes, I see.' She nodded, circling her. 'She might do. But that hair colour is way too obvious. Where did you get it, darling? Some ghastly place in the suburbs? You'll really have to get her some clothes, Tom, if you want to convince people.'

Cate flushed with annoyance as Tom Russell stood back to make his own assessment. 'Do you think so?' He put his head on one side to sweep a narrowed glance down to her ankles and up again. 'Still...' His cool, amused gaze locked with Cate's and her indignation flared. 'It might be best if you stay in the background until we can get you up to speed. People will only have to see us together once or twice to get the picture.'

Cate opened her mouth to retort, but Olivia interposed herself between them. She coaxed Tom a little aside and whispered, although Cate's smarting ears could pick up every word, 'But can she talk, darling? You know, if she's not a tiny bit educated, no one will believe it after Sandra.'

Tom Russell's black brows snapped together. A rebuke gathered in the air like a storm, until he glanced at Cate. Then his stern, sexy mouth relaxed. A reluctant smile crept into his eyes. 'The trouble is not whether she *can* talk...'

Olivia threw Cate a stony, narrow look, and placed a black-gloved hand on Tom's arm, positioning herself to give him an excellent view of her bosom. 'I'd love to stay for you, Thomas, but I'm afraid it's better I leave.' She added in a confiding voice, 'Malcolm's insisted on coming, and he's in a dangerous mood. I can't even bear being in the same room with him.' As if Cate were two paddocks away, she tossed, with a light, charming laugh, 'You'd better make it good, Dolly. We expect to get our money's worth.'

Cate's anger surged, but she held onto her temper. This was not the moment to offer herself as a rich woman's floor-wipe. She could admire Olivia's chutzpah, but didn't Cate Summerfield have her own distinctive brand?

Olivia needed to learn respect for the younger woman.

Cate smiled at the tabloid diva with angelic innocence and shrugged a shoulder. 'Certainly, ma'am. How about something like this?'

She flashed Tom a provocative glance and swept down her lashes. With a small seductive smile, she thrust a hip forward and sashayed over to him like some voluptuous sex siren. She stood as close as she dared, her body almost touching his.

She heard Olivia's sharp intake of breath, then the room grew still. Tom Russell seemed to freeze, as if his very nerve fibres had skidded to a halt.

Conscious of the blood pounding in her ears, Cate lifted her hand and lightly speared a tentative finger into the hard abdomen above his belt buckle.

He hardly appeared to breathe.

Pulsingly aware of the raw, masculine chest beneath the fine fabrics, she walked her fingers up his tie, then in mock feminine possession made a pretence of adjusting his shirt collar. She slid a languorous glance up at him through her lashes, then her lungs seized. His grey eyes clashed with hers, alight and blazingly sensual.

Unsmiling, he held her gaze for one breathless, scorching second, then in a swift, slick movement snaked his arms around her.

'Or this?' he said.

Before her shocked heart could slot back into its place he pressed his mouth to hers. She had little doubt it was calculated, but after the first stunned impact her lips sprang to tingling life as an electric charge vibrated through his big, lean body, and communicated itself to her like a primeval lightning bolt.

His charged fingers traced the length of her spine to her nape, then she felt him convulsively clench a handful of her hair in his fist. The conviction in that ruthless grasp was so electrifying, so risky, exhilaration flared in her blood like wildfire. Somehow the blaze must have infected him too, for he deepened the kiss to sizzling, sexual possession.

Her breasts swelled helplessly as the tip of his tongue slipped between her fiery lips to taste their inner softness. The sensation of his flicking tongue tantalising those tender tissues was so delicious and arousing, she was hardly aware of Olivia's outraged voice behind her and the snap of the door closing.

Drowning in their mingled breaths, intoxicated by the taste of him, the friction of his hard chest pressing her breasts, Cate was mesmerised, drunk on the sensual pleasures of his mouth, his knowing fingers and hard, muscled frame.

His hands surged to explore the curve of her hips, and her skin thrilled with a wild craving for more.

More of his lips. More of his clever hands. Beneath his increasingly bold caresses, her inflamed nipples and the intimate place between her thighs burned for his touch.

Suddenly she felt the hard evidence of his arousal push against her, then all too abruptly he broke the kiss and thrust her away from him.

She stared at him in shocked, panting upheaval. Naked lust flamed in the darkened eyes devouring her face, then he turned sharply from her.

Dragged from her swoon state, hot, flushed and dishevelled, her heart storming, she took moments to orient herself as rude reality flooded in and doused her fever. At least they were alone, she noticed with some relief.

She glanced confusedly at Tom's rigid back. His wide shoulders were set and tense, the hands at his sides balled into fists. Clearly he'd been as affected as she was. Tom Russell. Tom Russell and *her*.

Tom half turned and flicked her a glance that barely touched her. His grey eyes were forbidding, his face harsh and shuttered. When he spoke, there was nothing romantic about his tone.

'In case you've forgotten, today I am supposed to be honouring my dead father's memory.' Though his deep voice was quiet, its clipped tone cut her like a blade. 'I know how low your opinion of him was, but do you really think this is the day to be taking some slutty advantage of this situation? Have you *any* scruples?'

When the words sank through she gasped, 'Oh, that's—that is just—!' Her incoherent hands were fluttering at the injustice, her breasts rising and falling with indignation. 'Look, *I* didn't—it was you. I didn't want you to kiss me.'

'Is that why you struggled?' His sardonic eyes mocked her, and she flushed with shame at her undeniable compliance. 'I couldn't expect someone like you to know how it feels to have lost your only blood relative. Even so, you were willing to do more than just kiss me, weren't you? I've met more than my share of hungry little chancers who never miss an opportunity, but *this*…!' He shook his head in disbelief.

His contemptuous gaze seared her from head to toe. He strode to the door, then paused, his hand on the doorknob. The cold cynicism in his voice was crushing. 'Get one thing straight. Whatever dreams you might be cooking up in that scheming little head, I am *nothing* like my father.'

A saving wave of anger marshalled her brain cells. Trembling, she straightened her spine and advanced on him a step. 'Listen. You wanted to know if I could act. Well, that's what I was doing. Acting.' She hissed in a long, simmering breath and said in an unsteady voice, 'And get *this* straight. You can think yourself lucky to have taken me by surprise. Because I wouldn't kiss you for real if you were the last man in Australia.'

She swept past him and into the foyer. Following in her wake, Tom ground his teeth, trying not to watch her hair bounce and ripple in rhythm with her staccato motion. The feel of her smooth, supple flesh was still warm on his hands. And so alive. So dangerously, erotically alive. He had no choice now. He would have to keep her out of sight.

Out of *his* sight.

Dismay and self-disgust at his unaccountable behaviour roiled through him. The surrender to temptation had been bad enough. And as if it wasn't enough to find himself at the mercy of such a certified vixen, on this day of all days, how could he have been so reckless as to storm at her, so *inept*? Sure, he'd had to crush her pretensions, but how could he, Tom Russell, have acted so crudely? He'd offended her, and now he'd have to work that much harder to keep her to her end of the bargain. He clenched at the thought of having to crawl to her to make amends. Great bloody grief, he'd be forced to apologise.

The grim reality of his situation homed in on him, inciting an unfamiliar feeling of panic. He'd have to keep her away from people. In the mood she was in, God only knew what she might let slip.

A buzz of conversation burst upon them as, like two strangers, they approached the restaurant. Appetising food smells wafted from the kitchens, and despite her smouldering anger Cate's mouth watered, reminding her she'd skipped the boarding-house breakfast.

The dining room was set with silver and crystal, and flowed to a wide deck perched over the water. There the cream of Sydney society mingled, glasses in hand, raising their voices a little to hear each other over the hum they created in their gratitude at being released from the constraints of the cathedral.

It was an elegant assembly. The seasonal designer black was relieved by the occasional wink of diamonds; a jewelled bracelet glittered as a gloved hand flew up to protect hair from the breeze.

Some famous faces looked up from their conversations. Cate's anxious glance instantly lighted on a politician, who, that very morning, was gracing the front page of the *Clarion* over his possible links with a fraud scandal.

For a second her nerve nearly failed her. She looked uncertainly at Tom, and saw strain in the taut lines of his face.

Before they reached the deck he edged her into a quiet corner. He lifted his hands as though to touch her, then dropped them as if contact might mean instant electrocution. 'Look,' he said on a terse exhalation of breath, 'I overreacted. I should never have… Try to understand, I don't want any distractions today. All right? Can I trust you to stay here?'

She shrugged. Resentment burned in her chest like hot coals. Was a scoop worth it?

His jaw tightened. He gripped her forearm and bent his head to whisper, 'I'll make it worth your while. Whatever you want. Money…*any*thing.'

She looked witheringly down at his hand until he removed it. 'You don't have to offer me money. I don't go back on my word.'

A sharp flush darkened the tanned skin over his cheekbones. 'Oh.' He closed his eyes for an instant. 'All right, then. I—I beg your pardon. I—I'm sorry.'

The words sounded as if they'd been wrenched from him. She rolled her eyes and turned her face away.

He bit out, 'This won't take long.' In a gruff effort to placate her, he added, 'I promise I'll have you out of here as soon as possible. Now, remember—!' Bracing his wide, powerful shoulders, he gave her one last admonishing look, then strolled to greet his guests.

With a turbulent heart Cate watched him join the party. He wasn't nearly so overbearing to his guests. Before her eyes he morphed from a tense, arrogant control freak into Mr Smooth and Urbane.

With a handshake here, a few brisk words there, he welcomed them with the quiet civility expected of a sophisticated man suffering bereavement, and they clustered to him. Especially the women, she noticed, narrowing her eyes at the discreet elbowing for position among those anxious to lionise him under the guise of sympathy.

It was a polished performance, but she didn't feel like applauding. So what if he had a certain brusque sex appeal? The man had made her feel like a fool. Hell would freeze over before she'd ever kiss him again. She waited in her corner, a small proud smile fixed on her face to cover the mix of unpleasant emotions jangling in her chest.

Olivia's slur on her clothes stung, as did Tom's alacrity in agreeing to keep her apart from his friends. Her morning's confidence in her appearance was shot to pieces. Now, far from having a whimsical sort of chic, the second-hand suit seemed to scream its provenance.

Who did they all think they were? Just because she'd been brought up in a housing-commission house made her no less educated, no less civilised. Gran's house overflowed with books and music. Their friends were all people who valued ideas, culture, literature…

A few people nodded or spoke to her, but most just stared curiously and moved on. To make matters worse, Tom Russell's dark head kept turning to look at her. His every glance zinged through her like electricity, and challenged her nerves into a state of confused turmoil.

Checking to make sure she wasn't talking to anyone. It would serve him right if she pulled the plug.

Waiters flitted by with trays of fragrant, crispy morsels, but though hungry, she hesitated to try to catch any of their eyes for fear of attracting attention to herself. She noticed a couple of Tom's stepsisters peering her way, and made a strategic retreat, edging across the deck to a corner of the balustrade.

In an effort to blot him out of her awareness, she turned her back on him to lean on the rail and brood at the big white cruisers in the marina. But just as the fishy harbour smells couldn't destroy the aromas of garlic bread and balsamic dressing plucking at her stomach juices, neither could the picturesque charm of Sydney Harbour soothe her anger. The insult, the *insult* of being treated like a rich man's second-rate accessory.

How long before lunch was served and she could escape? Soon she would need to head back to the *Clarion* to compose her copy and sort through the morning's photos with Mike. She felt in her bag for her mobile, in hopes of sneaking a few surreptitious videos, then remembered Tom had it.

Blast. At least she'd have plenty to write about. She gave herself up to a satisfying rumination about the bombshell she could drop on Tom Russell if she had a mind to.

Why should she wait? She could have a fabulous scoop tomorrow. So let his merger fail. The man was ungrateful. Certainly, he knew how to kiss a woman, but that was where it ended. It was clear he had no idea of how to treat a girlfriend.

A pleasant male voice intruded on her reverie. 'You look like a thundercloud. Don't you like funerals?'

She turned to meet the enquiring gaze of a nondescript-looking man in his late thirties. He was smooth and pale, with eyes of a washed-out china blue and hair that had perhaps once been fair, but was now almost colourless, including that of his wispy little goatee. He sauntered over and placed his wineglass on the balustrade.

She replied coldly, 'Not especially.'

She angled slightly away from him and feigned interest in the progress of a ferry chugging towards the bridge, shielding her eyes, as much to exclude him as the sunlight dancing on the water.

Undiscouraged, the stranger said, 'Maybe they're an acquired taste.'

To her chagrin, he leaned both elbows on the balustrade. Settling in. All she needed now was for Tom Russell to notice and go berserk.

'I guess at your age you wouldn't have been to many,' he persevered. 'Is this your first?'

'No.'

Her cool tone drew a quick quizzical glance. Ashamed then of her unfriendliness, she unbent a little to explain, 'My first was when my parents died. I was five.'

He cast her an appraising look, and nodded. 'Well, after that, this must seem like a Sunday School picnic. How did they die?'

'Late at night on an icy road. We lived out near Orange then. It was a snowy winter.'

'Ah. Now that was tough.' He gazed thoughtfully at her, then his face broke in a smile. She didn't fancy goatees, but his pale blue eyes were tranquil and non-threatening, unlike Tom Russell's. There was no chance they could burn a woman to the ground one minute then freeze her to death the next.

She allowed herself to relax a little.

His gaze lit on her empty hands. 'Here, hasn't anyone given you a drink? What can I get you? Wine?'

'Oh.' She glanced across at the party crowd. Tom was in the midst of it, inclining his dark head to catch every last syllable from a skinny brunette who was eating him up with big, dumb, worshipping eyes. He'd forgotten about her already.

Without waiting for her reply the stranger raised a finger and a waiter materialised beside them with a trayful of drinks. She accepted the chill white wine with thanks, and took a grateful sip. It dropped into her empty stomach like acid.

'So,' her companion said, moving closer, his pale eyes luminous with concern, 'what happened to you after you lost your oldies? Who took you in?'

CHAPTER FIVE

THE TROUBLE with the women he met now, Tom brooded, attempting to disentangle himself from yet another bout of gushing hypocrisy, was their brazen sexiness. Sure, he enjoyed hot chicks as much as the next guy, but the women he really admired were cool, contained women, like Sandra. Women that a man needed to look into deeply to find their hidden qualities. Sandra had been perfect.

Well, apart from that one instance...

His gut tightened, though not with the same savagery he used to feel. He accepted now that it had all been his own fault. He'd been too caught up in the demands of the business. He'd been so focused on learning to keep his end of the corporation afloat that he'd neglected her. It was natural she'd drifted away.

So, apart from that one glitch... Though he still wondered sometimes if it had only been the one. There had been a distant look in her eyes more than once that had unsettled him.

Anyway, apart from that, Sandra had been close to perfect. She'd never driven him crazy, or made him furious, or made him want to strangle her.

Except after she was dead, and he'd found out the gut-wrenching truth of where she'd been driving down that midnight road. Then for a few brief minutes he'd wanted to kill her all over again with his bare hands, and—unbelievably—once or twice, himself.

But he was a civilised man, and he'd used his reason to detoxify those out-of-character responses, almost at once. And he'd mellowed. He had no lingering issues, with fidelity or otherwise. He was as faithful to her as he'd ever been. She was still the benchmark against whom he measured all women.

With Sandra, he'd never had to battle to concentrate on his work. So on a day like this, with the most difficult hand of cards a man had ever had to play, it was outrageous to have the distraction of a woman's slender, maddening form, just a few metres away, blazing in his consciousness like a beacon.

For God's sake, he had business to attend to. There was no putting off the afternoon's meetings with his lawyer and his stockbroker. Decisions had to be made, *today*. What was he to do about her while they were discussing which properties to throw on the market to raise some quick cash?

He disciplined himself not to glance at her. To cut her completely from his mind. The couple of times he'd been unable to resist had been a mistake. Though standing there in the corner all alone made her appear abandoned, even in some way vulnerable, he wasn't deceived.

That taunting little smile curving up her lips said it all. He was prepared to wager his last remaining assets that she was dreaming up vengeance. She probably couldn't wait to get back to her keyboard. Only the necessity of ascertaining whether rumours of his father's madness had begun to circulate the city boardrooms kept him from swooping down on her and whisking her out of harm's way at once.

He should never have brought her. But what else was he to have done to keep her away from the *Clarion*, apart from getting Timmins to lock her in his hotel room, bound and gagged? At once his imagination recoiled from the idea of Timmins manhandling her. No, he would have to have done the job himself. Tied her up. Handcuffed her, even. His imagination made a wild gratuitous leap to her spreadeagled on a bed, handcuffed to the bedposts...

The harping voices of some of his more powerful business associates filtered through, and he refocused. The essential thing was to glean what, if anything, they knew behind their bland smiles. All the time, though, a blonde time bomb, desirous of blowing him sky high, was ticking in his consciousness. The grim realisation dawned on him that he couldn't, under any circumstances, allow her to go back to the *Clarion*.

In the meantime, he'd have to find some way to placate her. For God's sake, she was a woman. Surely all he needed was to get her on her own. Take her to a place where he could soothe her ruffled feathers.

An intoxicating vision rose to fill his entire being, of him stroking her hair and her white throat as if she were a soft, pliant swan.

His mouth went dry. Tasting—he half closed his eyes—tasting the skin of her throat.

Unbuttoning her dress.

She'd be wearing underwear, of course—a lacy, flimsy bra, from which round pert breasts would burst like tender ripe fruit. She would quiver to his touch and…

A persistent plucking at his sleeve dragged him back to reality. With a start of irritation, he glanced down and saw it was the Prime Minister, eager to ingratiate himself. Sighing, he edged around slightly to position himself so he could keep an unobtrusive eye on Cate Summerfield over the shorter man's head.

He flicked a sideways glance across at her and felt a lurch of alarm.

She wasn't there!

He spun about to scan for her among the crowd, until the ominous silvery sound of her laugh drew his gaze past some shade umbrellas. Then something like a cannon ball blasted a hole through his insides.

Malcolm Devlin had her in his clutches. A small crowd was gathered around them, and she was chatting with people, flashing that smile, *laughing* in the presence of the most cunning bastard in the country.

Tom sucked some air back into his lungs. 'Not now,' he growled, shoving aside some irritating little pest who was blocking his path.

On an edge of anxiety, Cate half listened to the gossip swirling about her. At another time she'd have been tempted to whip out her notebook and dash down some of the choicer morsels. It was lucky she had an excellent memory for detail.

She'd intended to keep her promise not to talk to anyone, but how could she? By the time she'd realised who Malcolm was it was too late, and, before she knew it, to her dismay he'd attracted a crowd.

Fortunately, once she'd explained how she'd met Tom at a public hospital benefit, they had all started to look bored. She'd only had to start filling them in about the waiting list for heart surgery for most of them to find their own circle so riveting they forgot all about her.

Except Malcolm.

She glanced about for Tom, wondering with a nervous pang what he'd say if he caught her with Olivia's husband. She waited until the group around her were absorbed by the juicy topic of someone's fifty million dollar mansion, then made an effort to melt to the furthest corner of the deck.

To her intense annoyance, Malcolm Devlin followed her.

'Tell me again, Cate, what did you say your last name was?'

To a seasoned campaigner like herself, the innocence in his faded blue eyes was disturbing. His persistence was getting on her nerves.

She hesitated. 'Summerfield.'

His brow creased in thought. 'Summerfield,' he echoed slowly. 'Now where have I heard that name? Have you been in the social pages lately?'

The man had missed his calling. He'd have made a fine reporter. Cate rose up on her toes to look for Tom, but the view was obscured by some shade umbrellas. She moistened her lips. 'As a matter of fact…'

A tall black shadow loomed between her and the sun and her heart skidded to a giddy halt. Tom Russell, lean, dark and oozing menace, stood gazing down at her, and her pulse plunged into a mad, excited rhythm at the savage fire smouldering in his grey eyes.

His hands made a convulsive twitch towards her. 'Darling.' Though his tone was silken, the endearment speared a delicious thrill of fear down her spine.

With seeming difficulty, he dragged his eyes from her to her companion. 'Malcolm.' He thrust out a hand and the resulting handshake was like a sword clash. 'Good of you to come.'

Malcolm Devlin rescued his hand from the crush, flexing it by his side a couple of times to kick-start his circulation as he showered Tom with condolences. 'I've so enjoyed meeting your friend,' he continued when the spate had run out. 'Tell me, Cate, you aren't related to that Summerfield who writes for the *Clarion*, by any chance?'

Cate's nerves made an alarmed leap. She could feel Tom's burning gaze on her face, and noticed all at once that several people had drawn closer to listen, some of them Tom's relatives. Enough to constitute a lynch mob.

She felt an unaccustomed surge of panic. Malcolm Devlin had her on the rack.

She could lie, pretend she was another Cate Summerfield. It wasn't impossible that there would be others.

Then an image of Gran's wise, kind face rose in her mind's eye and she felt ashamed of her spineless impulse. How could she deny her profession, betray the ideals instilled in her since childhood? Tom's friends all valued their easy lives in their democracy, didn't they? How long did they think it would survive without the writers and thinkers who produced papers like the *Clarion*?

Despite her brave words to herself her coward's heart was

pounding like a jackhammer. Tom Russell would kill her. But she forced herself to meet Malcolm Devlin's malicious gaze, and screwed herself up for the truth.

'Yes, that's me,' she said, the barest tremor in her soft voice. 'I write for the *Clarion*.'

Though a proud smile was fixed to her face, the terrified hair stood up on the back of her neck. No one in the group stirred, struck dumb by the shock, perhaps. In a second they would recover, then lunge to seize her and string her up to the nearest yard-arm.

She was just considering doing a bolt when, with a deep internal gasp, she felt Tom's strong arm slide around her waist and draw her close. 'We're in the same business, aren't we, sweetheart?' He smiled down at her, though the smile didn't reach his glittering eyes. 'Just different ends of it.'

However self-serving his protective impulse, she was so thankful for it. She forgave him everything on the spot. Gazing up at him, she couldn't prevent her gratitude from bursting out in her warmest, most glowing smile.

It was astonishing how, even in a life-threatening situation, she could be so aware of the excitement of his big, masculine body in contact with hers. That lean, angular hardness ignited a sensual, pulsing blood-beat in her veins.

Perhaps the sensation flooded her brain, because even after they drew a little away from each other, she felt insulated against the sneers of Malcolm Devlin and his kind. Tom had in fact been speaking the truth. He and she were in the same business.

Unfortunately, their brief moment of connection didn't last. As the small group broke up and people drifted away one of Tom's stepmothers clutched at his wrist and said, 'It's good to see you with someone new, Tom.'

For an instant Tom Russell stilled. His lean, strong face grew rigid. Then he muttered a few polite, frozen words of farewell, grabbed Cate's arm and steered her through the dining room, where most people were now milling about and seating themselves. Heads turned in surprise, and some people waved and called goodbye to her as he hustled her straight past them, into the hall and out to the foyer.

As soon as they were out of earshot he spun around to confront her. 'Why did you have to tell people what you do?'

'Well, why shouldn't I? It's the truth. I have no reason to be ashamed of my profession.'

He raked her up and down with his smouldering gaze as if he'd like to rip her apart with his teeth. 'Do you honestly think Devlin…*anyone*…would believe I could be attracted to some hard, rapacious little dirt digger?'

Anger tore through her, hot and furious. 'Oh! The hypocrisy of that. I'm sure Malcolm knows as well as you do that there are fine and honourable people in journalism, as there are in every profession. Even *yours*. There are probably even some real journalists trying to fight their way through the sludge you expect them to churn out every day so you can rake in your billions.'

A muscle twitched in his lean, clenched jaw and she knew she'd hit home. But she was too fired up to stop there.

'And if you want to know if I think you could be… Yes! I think you could!'

His big body clenched, and his eyes flared with such anger she had to restrain herself from taking a backward step. Then he made a visible effort and controlled himself. He closed his eyes, and his jaw and the line of his wide shoulders relaxed. He breathed deeply several times and ran a hand through his pitch black hair.

After a few suspenseful seconds he opened his hands in a gesture of surrender. 'All right, all right, I apologise. I shouldn't have said those things. I'm sorry, honestly. I don't know what it is about me today…or *you*…' He exhaled slowly, then reached out and grazed her cheek with his knuckle. 'You know, I might just have to throttle you in the end.'

Before her mesmerised stare his expressive mouth edged

into a rare, reluctant grin. The grin warmed his eyes and crinkled them up at the corners, seeped through her skin like ultra-violet rays, and straight through all her defences. And when he took her arm and ushered her towards the door, she went with him like a lamb. A breathless, light-headed lamb.

He smiled down at her. 'So what *did* you and Malcolm talk about?'

'Hospital waiting lists.'

His eyes lit with laughter. 'I'm sure that's a subject he finds fascinating. What else, homeless people and the poor? I'd love to have seen his face.'

His amusement was genuine. As she took him in, sleek and elegant in his imported fabrics and handstitched shoes, it was clear he'd never been touched by poverty in his life. He'd never have to make do with accommodation in a boarding house so as to be near an ailing loved one. Neither he, nor Malcolm, nor any of their friends would ever know what it meant to struggle.

Despite the break in hostilities she felt a faint chill of depression. Never had she felt so far from home, not even when her parents had been buried and Gran had taken her over the Blue Mountains to Sydney. It was more than time for her to get back to the real world.

The glass doors slid open. With relief she saw the limo's long, sleek body drawn up before the entrance. 'Ah,' she said, striding for it, 'do you mind stopping on the way back to work so I can pick up a hot dog?'

About to open the car door, he paused, his eyes narrowed in calculation. 'What makes you think you're going back to work?'

She looked sharply at him. 'Well, I have to. I have to write my story and talk to Mike. I'm expected to file by five. And then there's—'

As if she hadn't spoken, he said, over her head, 'The hotel, Timmins.'

Rebellion rose up in her. She'd kept her part of the deal.

She just wanted to get back to her desk where she could think things through. 'But—

'No buts.' He urged her into the car. 'You and I need to talk.'

She resisted the pressure to get in. 'You seem to have forgotten I have a job to go to. And then I have to see my grandmother.'

'Bloody hell,' he said, throwing up his hands. 'Your grandmother, for God's sake. What does your grandmother have to do with anything?'

Well, hello *déjà vu*. She'd seen that look in a man's eyes before. It was the look she'd caught in Steve's whenever she'd had to cut short their time together so she could visit Gran. Exasperation, which in Steve's case had soon changed to contempt. It was crystal-clear that frail little old ladies were nothing but a nuisance to men with worlds to conquer.

A sound behind them drew her attention, and she saw with annoyance that Malcolm Devlin had just emerged from the glass doors. And, as if that weren't enough, the sly triumph of his expression made it clear he'd overheard.

He advanced on them, and opened his hands, his voice rich in bemusement. 'But, Tom,' he exclaimed, gazing from one to the other with apparent confusion, 'surely...*surely* you must know about Gran.'

Caught out! She felt herself blush bright red.

Tom Russell stood blinking rapidly for a minute, clearly thrown off guard. Malcolm advanced on them with a gloating, curious smile. 'How well did you say you know Cate?'

Cate gave Tom's sleeve an urgent tug, and he snapped from his momentary mental wanderings, and drew her to face him. 'We know each other, don't we, Cate?' he said.

The grey eyes frowning into hers were strangely intent. She made a sharp intake of breath as he bent his head and touched his lips to hers in a charged little sexy kiss.

Though brief, its erotic power was electrifying. Afterwards, fire-sparks still danced along her lips, and her breasts were left tingling and aroused. It was as though her body, having had one taste of him, could now be reignited by his slightest touch. And that seductive brush of his hand on her throat was so welcome to her weak flesh that as soon as it was gone her skin regretted its loss, and for a second she would have done anything, *anything*, to get it back.

Her heart was thundering so wildly she nearly stumbled from his grasp and into the car. He clambered neatly in after her, and lounged back against the cushions, his big, lean body angled towards her. Close. Far too close.

She fought to quell her seething pulse behind a cool face, crossed her ankles, clasped her trembling hands in her lap in a bid to seem composed and unaffected.

'Was that really necessary?' Her voice had turned hoarse.

'That trivial little performance?' He gave an amused shrug, and tucked some hair back behind her ear. If only the casual touch weren't so pleasurable to her skin.

How humiliating, to be so easily aroused to desire by a man who didn't approve of her. Who didn't even like her. Who was only *acting*. She really should get back to the safety of the newsroom. Immediately.

But Tom Russell's instructions were implacable. 'Hotel, Timmins.'

Hotel? What hotel?

The car started and purred forward. After a long, tense moment in which her heart's blood drummed a jungle beat, he leaned across to her and murmured, his voice tickling her ear, 'Did you know your eyes glow greener when you're excited?'

'Excited? Who's—excited? I was only acting.'

He gave a low, sexy laugh.

She felt an overwhelming need to arrest the pace before things veered wildly out of control, and directed her gaze through the darkened window at Malcolm Devlin. Malcolm was still standing in the same spot staring after them, with his head tilted to one side, stroking his flimsy little goatee, his pale eyes narrowed.

'That was a serious slip in front of Malcolm. Do you think he bought it?'

Tom Russell brought his sharp, intelligent gaze back to connect with hers. His eyes flicked to her mouth, then down to where her breasts rose and fell a little too fast beneath the cloth of her vintage Zampatti. 'I'm not sure he did. He *is* a very astute man. That's why it's imperative that we spend some time together now and work out some way of repairing the damage.'

Her heart skittered. 'But you do know—I can't stay long. I have to get back to my desk.'

His eyes veiled. 'Oh, I know.'

CHAPTER SIX

ORDINARY billionaires might live in houses or apartments. Tom Russell chose to reside in a hotel, though his was no sleazy downtown dive. It was a converted old maritime warehouse at the The Rocks, built on one of the piers which speared into Sydney Harbour. It had been part of a chain of so-called châteaux, this one designated the Château Bleu. While its interiors were light and modern, the high ceilings and cedar panelling in the ground floor rooms evoked its heritage.

She could see why it had been named Blue. Walking into the foyer was like boarding a ship. The wide windows revealed water views in almost every direction. As Cate approached the lifts the polished cedar floor seemed to shift and sway under her feet, in harmony with the gentle slap of waves against the pylons.

She accompanied Tom to a suite that appeared to occupy the entire third floor, her mind teeming with defensive ploys. She'd take care not to touch him. She'd avoid direct eye contact, and try not to argue, since it seemed to be their clashes that sparked the danger points.

As he opened the door and stood aside for her she hesitated, giving her watch a meaningful glance. 'I can only stay a few minutes.'

If she left now she'd just have time to write her story and file before she went to see Gran. 'There's my deadline, and then I must…'

She saw his eyes sharpen, and the words withered on her tongue. She'd already taken his measure about grandmothers. And after the care he'd been able to lavish on his father, with floating hospitals and personal physicians, she could imagine what he'd think of Autumn Leaves.

Tom heard the hesitation, and his curiosity was alerted. 'Must—?' he prompted.

'Oh, nothing…just—some things I have to do.'

He scrutinised her expression. Did she have a rendezvous planned for later? Her sensuous mouth was grave, the clear sea-green glance she cast him from beneath her lashes apparently innocent. She'd *said* she didn't have a boyfriend, but it was hard to believe guys wouldn't be queuing up.

But why would she lie? His instincts to believe the best of her battled with his intelligence. If he hadn't had first-hand knowledge of the deceits some women were capable of…

In spite of himself, though, his blood stirred, still fired with the effects of her sweet, wanton lips and their delicious surrender. Her response—and not once, *twice*—hadn't been his imagination. There'd been a hot synchronicity in the chemistry between them. Even now, the feel of her supple, vibrant body was still with him.

He watched her walk in ahead of him. As her graceful, feminine steps carried her through the hall her reflection bounced back at him from the mirrors on either side. He couldn't see her face in full, just the curve of her creamy cheek, but the impact was immediate. The distinctive tilt of her head, those cheekbones. His pulse made a leap. Volatile, dangerous, and…

He drew a deep, steadying breath. It seemed impossible that such a woman wouldn't have a lover. Wouldn't *need* a lover.

She cast a wary glance back at him, and a dangerous buoyancy arose in his blood, as if he'd had gallons of champagne to drink instead of the mineral water he'd kept to at the lunch. Cool down, he warned himself, aware of an urgent need to divest himself of his over-warm jacket. Chill. This was purely business.

Conscious of a heightening tension, Cate paused in the middle of a sitting room awash with blue light. It was furnished with massive sofas, curlicued couches, and soft, capacious armchairs.

Through a doorway off to her right a bedroom beckoned, its king-sized bed low, sleek and inviting. Piles of books spilled from the bedside tables onto the floor.

With the casual authority of a man in control of his territory, Tom Russell strolled across to open a column of windows beside wide balcony doors. Sounds from the harbour floated in on the salty air. He touched something, and cedar blinds switched silently down, reducing the views of bright water to enticing glimmers through the slats.

As the room dimmed it seemed to shrink, while Tom's presence loomed larger. The sea-laden air grew heavy with a languorous, intimate feel.

'Ah,' he said. 'Perfect.'

Perfect for what? An afternoon interlude between consenting adults? Was it her imagination, or was the air zinging with vibrations?

'This is very—spacious,' she said, extending her arms and twirling in an attempt to seem poised and in control. She came face to face with the doorway to the bed and turned quickly from it.

It was that first kiss that had done the damage. If she hadn't ever experienced his ability to raze her to the ground...

She glimpsed a mirrored dressing room larger than her room in the boarding house. There were racks of suits, shelves stacked with masculine apparel, and rows of shoes, all polished and immaculate. On the other side of the kitchen she saw a dining room, and beyond that a hallway to more rooms. 'Do you actually *live* here?' she exclaimed.

'Temporarily.' Tom Russell shrugged, slipping off his

jacket. Without it, the power and grace of his big, athletic frame was clearly apparent. She tried not to visualise the bronzed muscular arms and chest beneath his shirt. Focus on the Saturday edition, she warned herself. Concentrate on her responsibilities.

'Temporary until—when?' she enquired, noticing a stereo and stacks of CDs in one corner.

'Who knows?' He dropped some ice cubes into two glasses. 'Drink?' he said with a lazy, sensual glance.

Surely her imagination was going overboard? A highly respected businessman like Tom Russell wouldn't try to seduce her, just like that. 'No, no, thank you. I have to work, as you know. Soon. Very soon.'

He extracted a bottle of tonic from the fridge, poured some, then unfastened his tie and shirt collar. Her mouth dried, and she delved into her bag for her water bottle and took a quick swig. Surely he wasn't intending to undress?

In an effort to maintain the illusion that everything was calm and normal, she plunged into some bright, snappy chat. 'I had no idea you lived here. I—would've thought... All my colleagues seem to think you live in a mansion at Double Bay.'

He leaned against the bar, watching her replace her bottle with an ironic expression. 'That could be because I don't often feel a desire to confide in your colleagues.' His long fingers tightened on his glass, then, as though regretting his terseness, he added, 'They're probably thinking of my father's place. I don't—' He broke off, then shrugged and lowered his gaze to his drink. 'High stone walls and steel grilles are not to my taste.' He gave his glass an idle swirl, then glanced up at her. The edges of his mouth crept up a little. Was that challenge she could read in those steel grey eyes?

With his tie hanging loose he looked relaxed and seductive, like a big dangerous animal. A supremely confident dangerous animal.

Still, she could play it cool too, she thought with a wild pang. If he went as far as taking off his shirt she would walk to the door, make a dignified exit and dash for the lifts.

'Don't—get me wrong.' Though she tried to sound offhand, she could hear her awareness of him add unmistakable colour to her voice. 'This is a great suite, with the views and everything, but it's not exactly homey, is it? Aren't you worried about rising sea levels?'

'I live for the moment.'

'But don't you find it lonely?'

He smiled. 'It has all I need. A roof, and a bed.'

She cast the bed a sideways glance and gave a nervous laugh. In fact, she'd never seen so many gratuitously unnecessary places for lying down in one apartment. 'It certainly has that.'

He straightened up and strolled into his bedroom, drink in hand, his tall, lean sexiness still, for the moment, safely clothed.

'Anyway,' she persevered, to fill up the charged silence, 'the point I'm making…I mean, hasn't there been stuff written about this sort of thing? About how the homes that people choose are very significant? You know, for their emotional well-being, their psychology and all that?' He flicked an amused look back at her, and she swallowed. 'Wouldn't you like to have a home of your own? A house, or a flat?'

He set his glass down on a carved mahogany chest, sat casually on the end of the bed and slipped off his shoes.

'This is lovely,' she said huskily, hardly able to drag her eyes from his long, naked feet—how could a man's feet *be* so beautiful? 'But still very impersonal. And then there's your carbon footprint.'

He spread his hands in lazy acquiescence. 'I have a few houses here and there. Impersonal suits me fine. As for my footprint…' He extended a bronzed, elegant foot and inspected it with a bored expression, then shrugged.

She was staring at the gorgeous foot, trying to remind herself of how typical, how arrogant, how environmentally selfish the rich were, when he cast her one of those amused knowing glances that implied they had some shared understanding. Some deeply intimate mutual recognition.

Despite herself her heart thudded with an instinctive rush of acknowledgement. It was true, primitive instincts whispered all along her nerves. There was something in the air between them. It was like a highly incendiary spark that threatened to explode into flames at any moment.

Perhaps because her sexual sensors had overloaded her brain synapses, she hurried breathlessly on, 'But you must see the implication.'

'What implication?' He still smiled, but through his sleepy dark lashes his eyes sharpened.

In the effort to sound careless, her voice came out deeper than expected. 'Baggage.'

'Baggage!' His eyebrows swooped up and stayed hovering for an infinitesimal moment longer than they might have, before resuming control position. 'I have no baggage whatsoever.'

'Oh, right. I think men always say that. I find it impossible to believe someone could live beyond a certain number of years without *some* baggage. Surely everyone experiences a broken heart somewhere along the way, failed relationships...'

He tilted a sardonic eyebrow. 'Speaking from your wide experience?'

'Well...' Her hands fluttered around her. 'Certainly. I admit, I've had disappointments, although nothing of course, like your...your...' She felt herself begin to flush. 'I was actually engaged for a short time, quite recently.'

There was an alert little flicker in his eyes. 'How recently?'

'Well, perhaps not—not that recently. But it takes time to get over things, doesn't it?'

He considered her with his cool grey gaze for a long, nerve-racking moment, then with laconic ease rose to his feet. 'Would you excuse me while I get rid of these funeral clothes?' He strolled into his dressing room and closed the door.

She sagged, then tried some serious fast breathing to help herself get a grip. She could have groaned out loud. How could she have alluded to the loss of his wife like that, on the same day as his father's memorial service?

Still, she could hardly be blamed for being slightly off her usual game. It wasn't that she wasn't a sophisticated adult with enough worldly experience to hold her own with any drop-dead gorgeous man on his own ground. More that recent events had shaken her nerve. She put her fists to her cheeks, wondering if her long deprivation of masculine appreciation had driven her insane.

Anyway, if she'd wanted to kill the mood, her tactless words would have done the trick. She could almost certainly relax.

She moved over to the wall to study a framed pen-and-ink drawing of the stadium at the Sydney Cricket Ground. Another sport-crazed Aussie male, she grimaced to herself, then started as she heard him emerge from the dressing room. She turned and the breath was knocked out of her. The full animal impact of his gorgeous physicality hit her with adrenalising force.

He was wearing blue jeans and a white polo-shirt satisfyingly filled out by his bronzed, muscled arms and chest. He was all long, lean lines, wide in the shoulder, narrow at the waist and hip, coiled power in every honed muscle and sinew. At least, she thought, when her reeling insides had struggled back into recovery, his feet were now safely encased in leather and out of her lustful sight.

She glanced behind him into his dressing room and saw, beside a large laundry hamper, what looked like a wastepaper basket overflowing with something. She narrowed her eyes, trying to distinguish what it was. Surely that was his tie trailing on the floor. And wasn't that the sleeve of a shirt? With a curious sensation she realised that it must have been the clothes he'd been wearing.

He'd discarded them as if they were trash. Suit, shirt, everything.

With his long, lithe stride he prowled across the room to peer between the slats, then turned to lean idly back against the window to survey her, his hands resting on the sill either side of him. 'I've given it some thought, and I think the best way to be certain we've made up for that unfortunate slip is for us to invite Devlin over here tonight for dinner.'

'Tonight?' She tried to think, but it was hard to, in the presence of such raw, vibrant masculinity. 'But our agreement doesn't cover—the *night*.'

The word sounded so packed with sexual connotations she could barely restrain a blush.

Beneath his dark brows Tom Russell's eyes glinted. After a charged second he said, 'One of the terms of our agreement was to convince Devlin we're a couple. I don't think we can be sure we've achieved that.'

'But…I don't know if I can…*tonight*. I mean, what sort of thing were you suggesting?'

With the light behind him his eyes were as unsettling as a stormy sea, but his dark velvet voice reached her with quiet, measured potency. 'I think it's best if Malcolm sees you living here.' His eyes locked with hers across the room.

The wind was knocked out of her. She stared at him, incredulous. 'Living. You mean—sleeping? *Here?*' Her voice came out as a squeak.

'That's what it usually means.' There was the barest twitch to one corner of his sexy mouth.

'Oh, but—' she glanced about her, flinging out her hands '—this is small. Where would I sleep, here? What if it got out to the newsroom? My God, I'd lose my credibility.'

His big frame relaxed and he laughed with frank amusement, his eyes flickering over her. 'You're not exactly the most massive bulk I've ever accommodated. I'll find somewhere to fit you in. If necessary, Timmins can hunt up an extra bed.'

She shut her eyes briefly in an effort to think. *If necessary.* 'Timmins. Is Timmins here?' She threw a confused glance towards the foyer.

He shrugged. 'Somewhere. A few of my personal staff have rooms here.'

Visions of valets and shoe-shiners, maids and manicurists and silver-salvered butlers paraded through her boggling brain. His personal staff. 'But—what about the other guests? Don't you have security issues?'

He looked surprised. 'What other guests?'

She stared at him, marvelling at such unselfconscious complacency. He was so confident and satisfied with his rich man's lot. He could command whatever, whoever, he desired. 'Aren't you concerned about the tabloids having access to you here?'

A tinge of amusement crossed his face. 'Since I own most of them, no.' He gave a lazy wave of his hand. 'And don't worry about Olivia's. I'll make sure they aren't a problem. Your friends will never have to know you're living with me.'

She ignored the sardonic inflection. It was the last bit that stuck.

Living with him.

As soon as the words were out sultry images insinuated themselves into her imagination. Lying naked in his arms. Kissing and more kissing…The dark heat, the passion…

She clasped her hands tightly in front of her. 'No. No, look, I don't think so. If you had a house like normal people, I might risk it. But I can't see myself in this *suite*, at night with all this—' she made a sweeping indication of Sydney Harbour glimmering through the blinds '—and your staff—and *you,* and…'

Tom Russell rubbed his ear. 'Look at it this way. You want your interview—I want Olivia to go on with the merger. It's in both our interests to persuade Devlin that we're lovers. Can you think of a more effective way?' Despite his lazy posture, his tone managed to be quietly forceful. 'It would be a pity to lose this opportunity.'

'We-e-ll…' She drew a long quivery breath. 'I don't know. Although…perhaps for one night. If it's the only way.' Thoughts of those kisses, still warm on her lips, and her eager, uncontrolled responses, seethed in her mind. 'But only if you promise on your absolute, sacred honour, cross your heart and hope to die, not to…on no *account* to try to—to—' She broke off to drag in an agitated breath.

His brows shot up in amused surprise. 'To what?' He scored her face with his sharp, intelligent gaze, then strolled over and gripped her shoulders. Her thudding heart began to race as he said softly, 'You're not as cool as you pretend, are you, Goldilocks? Do I make you nervous?'

'No,' she blustered. 'Of course not. Why would I—? How—how ridiculous…'

He frowned, studying her face, then said almost dreamily, 'I think you need to calm down.' His eyes shimmered into hers, as mysterious and affecting as the sea at first light, then he raised his hand to smooth her hair back from her temples.

The touch of his fingertips on her skin sparked a shock wave through her nerves, but when he spoke his deep voice had a hypnotic, soothing quality. 'Just relax. When you do you'll see that this is an obvious and necessary part of our deal. Sleeping here isn't such a frightening thought, is it?'

'Well, no, but—'

'Shh, now.' He placed his finger over her lips, and she held her breath. The sensual light in his eyes intensified as he stroked the hair from her forehead with a mesmeric rhythm. 'You seem very tense,' he soothed. 'Just let yourself chill.'

Chill? How could she chill? He was so achingly close, the mingled scents of his clean male skin and freshly laundered clothes filled her head, stirred her senses and made her blood race until she was unbelievably *hot*. A virile little pulse was beating in the strong, bronzed column of his neck. Somehow, the sight of it trapped the very breath in her throat.

'If we're to convince anyone,' he murmured, 'it's important for us to become used to touching each other. Body language is such a telling form of communication.'

He was so persuasive, his stunning eyes so piercing and compelling, that when he slid his hands into her hair and fiery little tingles crept all over her scalp, she didn't argue. She closed her eyes to savour the sensation.

His fingers caressed her nape with a tenderness that imposed a delicious paralysis on her limbs. The silence was disturbed only by her heartbeat and occasional sounds from outside. There was the muted hoot of a ferry, then the room fell preternaturally still.

Her senses spun in a tumultuous confusion, and she opened her mouth to tell him something important she had to do, then forgot what it was because his hand slipped to her throat and, as if she were made of silk, caressed her skin with soft, sensual strokes.

Time stood still. Shivery sensations trailed from his fingertips. She stood spellbound, immobilised by the seductive magic of his touch, electricity thrilling into her face and hair.

He drew her closer into his strong, hard body, and the intoxicating scents of him, the sound of his intense, rapt breathing—or was it hers?—mounted in her senses, and kindled that wildfire in her blood she'd been fighting all day. Like the weak traitors they were, her lips burned for another taste of his firm, masculine mouth.

'Your skin is so amazingly delicate,' he said thickly, and bent to sear her throat with a kiss. A deep gasp of pleasure escaped her.

With a thundering heart she felt his fingers slide below her neckline to release the top button of her jacket, and her breasts swelled in helpless erotic anticipation. But paradoxically, for some reason, even as her shameless flesh warmed with enthusiasm to the unfolding scenario, the sweet narcosis in her brain cleared.

Time was marching on. She had a story to file, and a little old lady expecting her at six. Swiftly she grabbed Tom Russell's hands to still them, and gave him a determined shove. 'Look,' she said hoarsely, backing away from him, 'I have to go.'

As he stood blinking at her in the charged silence with apparent surprise, questions began to crowd in on her. What had he intended, stroking her like that? Was it just some weird impulse he'd given way to, or a calculated delaying device? Would he have actually gone all the way to *seducing* her?

When he spoke, his breath coming rather quickly, there was gruffness in his deep voice. 'Sure, sure, of course.' He ran his hand through his hair a couple of times, possibly to give his cool time to recover. 'I'll—I'll drive you back.' Then, as though in denial of anything outrageous having happened, he strolled across to a cabinet, and took some keys from a drawer.

She shook her head, confused and astonished by her own compliance, wondering if she should give herself a good, sound pinching. She'd come close to being hypnotised. What was he—a snake-charmer?

Hastily she tidied herself, ensuring that all her buttons were secure. 'This—is exactly the sort of thing I mean,' she said, her voice husky and tremulous. 'I hope you aren't trying to claim that what happened just now was part of the deal.'

His powerful frame tensed, then he turned to face her, the shadowed eyes below his black brows unreadable. 'What happened, though?' he said softly.

'*What* happened? Well, you—you stroked my neck. You were caressing my hair.'

'Caressing?' His eyes sparked in denial. 'I most certainly was not *caressing*, as you call it. I was merely calming you down.'

She could hardly believe her ears. He should have been a politician. His expression was bland, but there was no way she could be bamboozled by a man who had now kissed her *three times*.

'But—that kiss on my neck. What do you call that?'

He lifted his brows. 'I call it a reluctant, but graceful acceptance of our need to become more familiar with each other.'

She was about to deliver a caustic retort when a phone started ringing, and he smoothly excused himself and strode into his study.

She located her bag on a small side table in the hall, and plunged into its depths in search of her hairbrush, still conscious of his touch lingering on her skin. She needed to be alone to do some hard thinking.

After a short while he came back, his brows drawn in satirical amusement. 'That was Devlin, checking up. But fine. He's agreed to come.' He made a wry face. 'I knew he would. Just try keeping him away.' He noticed her clicking her bag shut. 'In fact, you don't have to leave at all, do you? You can use my study to write your blurb. We should make some sort of action plan, so why not email your piece? It'll give us time to talk.'

It sounded almost reasonable, but then he gave his brows a suggestive lilt that gave her a severe jolt. The faintest of smiles began to curl the edges of his chiselled, sexy mouth.

Her blood, still heavy with the power of his touch, beat confusedly in her ears. What did he really intend? Was he trying to tempt her into an afternoon of love-making? Against her will, against all the urgings of her intelligence, she felt the treacherous flame leap in her veins. Somehow, though, her conscience managed to assert itself. She could imagine Harry's reaction if he knew she'd typed her Russell story on Tom Russell's keyboard.

'You know I can't.' Her voice came out with an annoying huskiness.

'Why not? Surely journalists do that all the time.'

'They do, of course, but I'm…' She hesitated. How safe would it be to reveal to him, of all people, her lowly status in the scheme of things? Although why should she care what he thought of her? She was hardly trying to impress him, was she?

His brows lifted interrogatively. She felt the faint colour warm her cheeks, but met his gaze coolly enough. 'Well, actually… This is my first news story. I expect Harry might want to talk about it with me. I don't want to disappoint him. And I'll need to go through the photos with Mike.'

'Ah.' His black brows shot up again. 'Your first break. So this is a big day for you?'

She made a stiff, self-conscious nod.

His eyes dwelt thoughtfully on her face. Was she imagining it, or did they have a softer light? Suddenly he looked kind, almost sympathetic. 'So…would Harry be Harry Fitzgerald?'

Her jaw dropped. 'Do you *know* him?'

'Of course. We're in the same business. He's a good man, Harry. I think I know most of your bosses—and you'd be surprised how much about your reporters.' He wrinkled his brow in thought. 'What's the name of your boy wonder, now? The guy with the ginger hair? Wilson, isn't it?'

She acknowledged it with a slight nod. 'Steve.' She'd loved to have seen Steve's face at being described as a boy.

'That's right. I do try to keep an eye on my competitors.' He threw her an amused glance. 'You know Harry worked for my father once?'

'*Did* he?'

She could scarcely believe her ears. Wait till she told Marge. And to think that Tom knew so much about the *Clarion*. She couldn't help looking at him with more respect. Suddenly their separate news worlds seemed more connected than she'd thought.

He smiled, and the smile crept into his eyes. 'I hope that doesn't turn you off him.'

She acknowledged the dig with a small laugh, and as their glances meshed in a rare cosmic moment of shared appreciation pleasure surged in her heart. The lines around his eyes and mouth were alive with sudden humour, and she was seized with a breathless desire to hold things still, to stay bathed in the warmth of his smile, savour his deep laugh…

Regretfully, though, she had to tear herself away. She picked up her bag and slung it on her shoulder. His eyes sharpened and followed the movement.

He strolled over to her, standing idly with his weight on one foot, his hands loosely tucked into his jeans pockets. 'I can see why you're so anxious to rush back and write your story.' His tone was very, very casual. 'Covering the memorial was of great importance to you, personally.'

She nodded, wary at a sudden tension she sensed in him.

'It must be quite a temptation to report everything. All that you overheard.'

'No, no,' she hastened to reassure him. 'The memorial itself is a great story. I'm aware the private stuff is off the record. The legal boys probably wouldn't even let me use it. And if I know I'll have the big scoop at the end…'

'And you will.' He smiled, but his eyes were unreadable. He added, as if he'd only just thought of it, 'You *could* phone your copy in, though, couldn't you?'

She gave a light laugh to disguise her unease. 'I hope you're not trying to keep me away from my desk. You can't lock me up and keep me prisoner, you know.' She saw him flick a glance towards the outer door, and wondered with a small shock if he'd considered doing just that. She added softly, 'You'll have to trust me, won't you?'

He didn't answer, but a tiny involuntary flicker of his black lashes said it all.

An ominous truth dawned on her. No way did he trust her. Not in the slightest.

Phones started ringing, several phones, all shrieking at the same time. He hung there poised, glancing from her to the door with a narrowed gaze—measuring the distance?—then with a muttered curse sprang to deal with them.

Perhaps she had been momentarily beguiled, but her brain hadn't quite lost it. If Tom Russell was dreaming of locking her up, he could forget it.

She made a dash to the front door, dragged it open, and, vacillating between the lift and the stairs for less than a nano-second, was in the lift pressing the button for ground before the heavy door even had time to click shut.

Quickly, quickly, she willed the lift doors, in a torture of suspense as they took an eternity to glide across. An instant before they met, her frantic gaze caught the flash of his dark figure racing towards the stairs.

CHAPTER SEVEN

THE LOBBY seemed quiet. At one end the concierge leaned on his lectern, chatting with a security guard. As Cate burst from the lift to flee for the entrance she saw them look up in surprise. Although in a fever of expection of Tom Russell's hot breath searing the back of her neck at any second, she thought it prudent to slow a little, and flashed them a friendly glance to allay any suspicions.

They smiled uncertainly, then the smiles froze on their faces. She noticed the guard snap up straight and move sharply away from the desk, while the concierge's gaze seemed to be captured by something behind her.

Someone.

A strong, lean hand closed around her upper arm and her heart jarred in her chest.

'You didn't say goodbye,' Tom Russell said, spinning her around to face him.

She was panting, partly from the exertion of dashing, and partly from the strange exhilaration of being physically pursued by an attractive and dangerously sexy man. Even after he'd raced down several flights of stairs *his* breathing was as even and controlled as a somnolent lion's. He tossed some car keys to the concierge over her head, then turned back to grill her with his smouldering gaze. She had the sensation of being bathed in a shower of sparks.

'No, well…' she said, wilting to the stern accusation in his compressed and sensually stirring mouth, 'I was feeling queasy. I'm actually very susceptible to seasickness, and this building does churn about, doesn't it?' She dragged in some air. 'As well as that, you were…so busy with all your important calls, I didn't want to intrude on your private business affairs.'

He looked sceptical. 'Since when?'

It was a cynical gibe, but she let him get away with it. 'Anyway,' she added, 'you know I'm in a hurry to get back. I thought if I took a taxi it would save time.'

His eyes grew reproachful, as if he were completely innocent of abducting her with the intention of making her his prisoner, and probably his sex-slave. She felt a qualm of doubt. Had she been unfair to mistrust him?

'I can drive you there before you can even say *taxi*,' he said tightly, almost spitting the word. 'Unless you don't trust me to?'

Though he was no longer gripping her arm, his chest was practically grazing her nipples, swelling her bra to bursting point and rendering her knees strangely weak. She was breathlessly alive to the persuasive power of his bronzed, muscular arms, her chances of making a break seemed slim.

'Oh. No, no, it's not a matter of trust. Of course I—I *trust* you…'

His mouth only made the tiniest curl, but it was so potently expressive of disbelief.

She was racking her brains for a neat way out when she noticed his eyes shift, then light with satisfaction. Following their direction she saw a sleek, sporty car sweeping into the driveway. Emblazoned on its red mudguard was a prancing horse, almost certainly a stallion. Tom Russell overrode her protestations about hailing a filthy taxi. He hustled her outside and deposited her into the car's deep leather passenger seat, then strode around to assume the driver's seat.

'I know this can be difficult for a woman,' he said grimly, firing the ignition, then easing them down the driveway and into the traffic stream, 'particularly one in your profession, but I expect people to be straight with me. If you had no intention of honouring your end of the deal, you should have said so.'

She gasped and retorted, 'I did—I *do* intend to honour it.'

'My point being,' he continued in a measured, chilly tone as if she hadn't spoken, 'that with all the life-and-death matters screaming for my immediate, urgent attention, so far I've dedicated most of this day to you. I had even started to believe that there was some sort of rapport happening. But after your astounding exit, how can you expect me to trust you?'

'Oh, for goodness' sake,' she snapped, to cover a degree of guilt. 'I explained why I did that. You know very well I'm in a hurry to get back to work. I've wasted enough time as it is.' She glowered mutinously ahead. 'Haven't I already agreed not to report your conversation with Olivia? You should learn to trust people.' An upcoming traffic light exacerbated her frustration. 'Can't this thing go any faster?'

There was a brief, appalled silence. 'This—Ferrari?'

He made a smooth, deliberate gear change, put his foot down, and whizzed the machine through the intersection, then, as if to taunt her, wove it with giddy, split-second timing, in and out between the lanes, speeding down a confusing series of streets, alleys and narrow old byways until she had no idea where they were.

She refused to be impressed. 'It must be dreadful to have a pretty toy like this and still be stuck with having to drive it through the same shabby old streets and grimy old buildings as everyone else.'

'Not at all,' he said politely. 'I happen to love these shabby old streets. I find these grimy old buildings quite beautiful.'

How did he manage to make her feel like a snark? Scanning the current streetscape, she supposed some of them could be considered beautiful for anyone rich enough to have the time to look at them. Now that he'd mentioned it, it was as if she were seeing them for the first time.

In fact…

She peered anxiously about. She wasn't familiar with much more of the city precinct than the shopping streets and those that were visible from the train she caught to work, but weren't they travelling *away* from the *Clarion*? Surely now they were heading east. She strained to see some landmarks and to read the lettering on the shop fronts. She should have been able to see Chinatown by now. With a lurch she realised that the city towers were gradually giving way to lesser buildings and maritime factories. 'I don't know this route. Isn't this Woolloomooloo?'

'It's a short cut.'

She felt a pang of alarm. Wasn't that what kidnappers always told their victims? She glanced at him, but his harsh profile was inscrutable, his mouth firm and controlled.

Of course, she reflected with growing certainty, how could he risk her spilling the beans? He knew she'd be weighing up the chances of her scoop going cold, of circumstances changing and it all whittling away to nothing. In his shoes she'd do the very same thing. Where would he be taking her? She couldn't help thinking of that house with high stone walls and steel grilles.

A shameful surge of excitement swept through her at the things he might intend to do with her there, but she sternly repressed it. As lean, gorgeous and addictive as Tom Russell was proving to be, she was in charge of her destiny, *and* any physical clashes she might choose to engage in.

She considered her narrow range of options. If she wanted to file her story there was no choice but to open the door and jump out at the first opportunity. An intersection was coming up, and she tensed as the traffic light flicked to orange. She eased open her seat belt catch with one hand, and inched the other to the door handle. A tentative tug revealed it was locked.

Blast. The car's smooth, gleaming luxury closed in around her like an implacable prison. There had to be a way. Her roving glance alighted on the pristine carpet beneath her feet. In a wave of what must have been divine inspiration, she plunged into her bag for a handful of tissues and pressed them to her mouth.

'Do you mind stopping here? I think I'm going to be sick.'

'What?' The word was wrenched from the depths of him. He swivelled around to stare at her in disbelief. 'Is this for real?'

She gazed wanly at him and dredged up a sick little cough.

With a muttered exclamation, he twisted around to look for a break in the traffic, then swerved across a lane and skidded into the kerb, halting before the striped awning of a row of shops.

He leaned an arm on the wheel, studying her with amused suspicion. 'It can't be the motion of the car. This vehicle was custom-built to give the smoothest possible ride.'

'Please,' she choked, rolling him a distressed glance. 'The door.'

His brows edged further together. 'Though I s'pose... you did say...'

She put her hand over her mouth and made a convulsive heave. Alarm shot into his eyes, and he swiftly released the central lock. The instant she heard the click, she opened the door, flailed her way out of the seat belt, and in her panic nearly fell onto the pavement, dragging herself upright just in time to avoid crashing into a bunch of afternoon shoppers.

The nearest shop entrance was crowded with a display of Eastern carpets. Recovering her balance, she ran for it, dimly conscious of the sound behind her of Tom's door closing.

'Sorry,' she gasped, colliding with a fat teenager buried in a drink carton.

Barely avoiding a rack of clothes a man was pushing along the street, she raced past the warehouse doorway, and fled into the entrance of a neighbouring arcade. The mall promised to stretch to the next street, but, knowing how easily Tom could catch her on the straight with his long athletic stride, a third of the way along she veered into a shop door, and found herself inside the rug warehouse.

The vast musty interior smelled of dust and exotic places. It was crammed with enormous racks of ceiling-to-floor rugs, piles of Indian dhurries and carpets in massive rolls—a perfect maze of hiding places.

She crept behind a suspension stand of Pakistani rugs, waiting for several heart-thundering minutes for Tom to pounce on her from behind like a slavering wolf. When her wild pulse had calmed a little and she judged he'd have given up her pursuit and driven off, she stole back towards the entrance, and peered between the carpets in the front windows.

Her lungs seized. He was still there, standing by the kerb, scanning the street, anxious impatience in every line of his big, lean body. She watched him glance at his watch and pace to the entrance to the arcade to stare down its length. He moved so close to the window she could see the sexy shadow under the taut skin of his jaw. She shrank further back behind the display, fearful he'd somehow realise she was on the other side of the glass.

After a few more minutes he returned to the car, but he didn't drive away. It homed guiltily in on her that he was waiting. Waiting for her to come back from whatever private sanctuary she'd sought. Giving her time. Allowing her privacy.

Believing her.

Her urgency to flee down that arcade into the next block, find a taxi, and speed to work warred with a sneaking sympathy for Tom Russell and the low trick she'd played.

She was almost overwhelmingly tempted to run to him and explain. Although, she argued with herself, even if he did believe she was ill, he'd still intended to abduct her. This dangerous weakness she was developing for him was beginning to look like Stockholm Syndrome, and there was only one way to fight it. She had to walk away. Run, in fact.

She did run, down the arcade to the next street, where she hailed a passing taxi. The driver made a neat U-turn, then drove her back towards the city's heart, and the *Clarion*. The trouble was that every kilometre away from Tom Russell was a ridiculous, tearing wrench.

CHAPTER EIGHT

AH-H-H...COFFEE.

The essential newsroom aroma infiltrated Cate's tissues and her hunger, temporarily suspended by serial rushes of adrenaline, came roaring back.

Lunch would have been cleared away by now in the cafeteria, but there were bound to be sausage rolls down in the warming-oven. Her mouth watered at a tantalising vision of their aromatic succulence wrapped in buttery, flaky pastry. If she could bring one back to her desk, she could see Mike, write her story, dash to Gran, and then...

Then...?

Go home. Go home, and...what? *Pack?*

She closed her eyes as her insides clenched into an excited knot. Would she—*could* she seriously contemplate going back to Tom Russell?

She glanced almost furtively across the busy newsroom, hoping the fever seething in her veins didn't show. Everyone appeared intent on their work. How many of her colleagues, she wondered, were harbouring secrets that could blow the country sky-high?

While amazing things had happened to her, and she had an exhilarating sensation of rushing towards a precipice at breakneck speed, around her life was continuing with the same buzz as was usual at this time every day. People were at their keyboards, hastening to meet their five o'clock deadlines. The sub-editors were hunched over copy, poised to strike out offending phrases.

She spotted Mike, sprawled back in his chair with his feet up on the desk, and put her need for food on hold while she threaded her way through the aisles for a look at his pictures.

He accepted her apology for failing to connect earlier with an easygoing shrug, and good-naturedly removed his feet from the desk and made room for her. He'd already edited his best shots, and had set up a clever composite of celebrities arriving at and departing from the church. She drew up a chair and let him scroll her through the elegant selection he intended to pass on to his editor.

There was a compelling close-up of Tom, caught unawares in the church car park before the service. She stared at it for seconds, and halted Mike when he would have clicked on further. Tom's unguarded expression was so strained and grim, she was seized with a renewed sense of the desperation that had hung about him in the church.

It was no game he was playing, she realised. His contract with her was serious. Deadly serious. He was counting on her.

With a pang of apprehension it occurred to her that after her mad dash to escape, he might assume she was planning to renege. She remembered his cool threat to spill the merger himself. That would be such a desperate move. Proud, ruthless and hopeless. It was clear Russell Inc was in trouble. *Tom* was in trouble. She should contact him. Let him know what she intended.

Although, what did she intend?

She finished with Mike, then headed for the cafeteria, absorbed in her dilemma. Certainly she'd made a deal, but, immersed once more in the solid reality of the newsroom, it was hard to contemplate not revealing what she knew about the merger at once. The revelation would be such a coup for the *Clarion*. But could she really contemplate breaking her word to Tom Russell? Her heart flinched from such a betrayal.

She wondered how many of her colleagues had held back on stories because of personal loyalties. Most of them were kind, decent people. Knowing them as she did, she felt sure such things must often happen, despite the bosses' insistence that friendship must be one thing, business something else entirely.

Still, she had to face it that in a moral sense honest, objective reporting was her first responsibility, to the paper and to the nation.

But how moral would it be to harm him for the sake of a story, no matter how newsworthy?

Although, what if the story leaked and another reporter scooped her? Or what if Tom failed to keep his side of the bargain? Did he even deserve that she should keep hers?

He'd intended to seduce her—or had he? He'd certainly intended to delay her. He'd shown a ruthless disregard for her. Insulting her, kissing her like that, pursuing her like a furious wolf, attempting to abduct her…

Just thinking about it sent a rush of excitement through her veins like electricity.

As she paid the cashier and started back for the newsroom she made an effort to calm her turmoil and think. Tom was no fool. Hadn't they all told her what a tough operator he was? He was good, she had to give him that. In some subtle way he'd made her feel so feminine and desirable, she'd been mesmerised.

Wasn't that the real danger? If a man could persuade her to let him stroke her very *neck*, what else could he persuade her to do? A neck might not have the same intimate status as a breast, or a thigh, but coming so soon after a kiss—two kisses, to be exact—there had been something undeniably sexual about it. If she hadn't stopped him, who knew how much further that little situation could have developed?

With her history, the solution was obvious. She should never see him again. Except...

She couldn't remember ever feeling so *alive*, as if she were in some zesty contest with him. Couldn't she allow herself a little bit of fun? If he'd been truly sinister and willing to cause her harm, would he have stood back and waited for her after he'd let her out of the car? She bit her lip, wondering what he'd be thinking about her now, then broke into a smile. With his temper, he was probably fantasising about murdering her.

One thing was certain, she reflected as she approached her desk, if she blew the gaff on his merger, she could never face him again. She'd feel as if she had a blot on her soul a mile deep. But if she kept her part of the bargain...if she went back...if she actually stayed overnight with him...

She bumped into her chair and coffee sloshed from her paper cup. Marge was back at her desk, she noticed, watching her with a curious little crease between her brows.

'Oops.' She flashed Marge a grin.

Ignoring her friend's scrutiny, she sat down. What was Marge staring at, anyway? She sipped her coffee, parked her sausage roll, and faced her empty screen.

Where to begin? What she needed was an angle. Some way to report on the event, while illuminating a measure of the man who was the true story at its centre.

Her desk phone rang. Absently she picked it up. 'Yes?'

'Cate.'

The deep dark voice flooded her being. She froze on the edge of her chair, gripping the phone. Stay calm, she warned her mad pulse. Stay in control.

'What?' she breathed when her lungs would allow it.

'You panicked.' The quiet mocking charm of Tom Russell's tone, as if in acknowledgement of the sexy contest between them, thrilled through her like an ocean wave. He wasn't furious.

'I did not,' she retorted, then, realising she was grinning, angled her face away from Marge's line of vision and said in a low, husky murmur, 'I most certainly did not panic. I simply took prudent evasive action.'

'From what? What scared you?' There was genuine enquiry in his voice.

'If you must know, I object to being kidnapped.'

'Kidnapped!' He sounded astonished, as if kidnapping were a remote, undreamed-of concept. 'Are you serious? You mean—just now in the Ferrari? But how the hell—? What gave you that idea?'

She felt a tiny doubt, but it was almost instantly replaced by recognition. Such sincerity. What brilliant liars men could be.

'Let's just say I sensed it, Tom.'

'Ah. You sensed it.'

She could hear the smile in his voice, and despite her indignation with him warmth radiated through her and swelled her breasts.

She pressed her inner thighs together and clung to the phone, drinking in his silence, almost able to hear his brain cells ticking over. Eventually he said very softly in his dark velvet voice, 'I think we both know that wasn't what you were scared of, sweetheart. But don't forget we have a deal. I'll pick you up at home. Where exactly do you live?'

'*God*, no.' She imagined him driving up to the boarding house, witnessing the humble reality of her temporary abode, and her insides shrivelled. He'd probably think he was in some parallel universe. 'You mustn't do that. Please,' she added with heartfelt urgency, then lowered her voice to a whisper, 'I'll come to the hotel.'

The silence crackled with tension. Struggling, she guessed. His need to have control versus his need to keep her sweet.

'If you can't trust me to come there by myself then you can't trust me at all and we'd better call everything off,' she blurted, then waited, trembling, her fingers crossed that she hadn't pushed his machismo too far.

'Be here by seven or I'll know you're breaking your word and I'll sink the merger.'

The last uncompromising words were said with finality, as if he were about to hang up, and she cut in swiftly, 'No, no, I can't be there by seven. I have to... Make it eight-thirty.'

'Seven-thirty.' He disconnected before she could argue.

Seven-thirty. She unglued her sweaty fingers from the phone and slumped back in her chair, aware of a roaring in her ears. But her chaos wasn't about having the power to change the corporate history of the nation's newspapers, or even about the things she had to accomplish before seven thirty. It was the effect of that casual observation.

We both know that wasn't what you were scared of.

She rested her elbows on the desk, her fingers over her ears to cool them. Was he toying with her? Using his sexual power to manipulate her? Or could romance be on the agenda again? He wouldn't have made that cool reference to the attraction if he wasn't as aware of it as she was. But the risks involved... A man in her life—and *such* a man...

She felt another wave of excitement, and, with a reinvigorated sense of his masculine essence, her fingers hovered, tingling with juice, over the keys. What to say about him? He was aggression, he was fury, he was charm, he was humour, he was...she closed her eyes, savouring the memory of his rich, seductive voice. *Sweetheart.* Had that been an endearment?

Once she made a start, her copy flowed like honey. Fortunately for her narrow time frame, she'd already composed much of it in her head during the intervals between tumultuous events.

In the midst of the newsroom's habitual, last-minute frenzy to pull things together, the news editor found the time to examine it, fire a few searching questions at her, then slash a red pencil through several lines of the second paragraph before passing it on to the world-weary sub-editor for more gratuitous slashing. She hoped he wouldn't ruin it, but if there was a chance they might find a spot for her lead-in on the front page she'd accept any changes as worth it. That it would be the Saturday edition would be even more gratifying.

She would have loved to stay and eavesdrop on the conference to finalise the competing stories for page one, but she was running late. It was out of her hands.

On the train to North Sydney she considered how much it would be safe to tell Gran about the memorial. If Gran had the slightest inkling of her attraction to Marcus Russell's son… It could kill her, Cate realised with cold certainty. At the very least she'd worry so much there could be a serious downturn in her health.

It was nearly six-thirty when she hurried into the ward. To her remorse she saw that Gran was having one of her breathless days. No one had helped her to sit up, so, imprisoned by her weakened lungs and labouring heart, she was still prostrate on her mattress. Her meal was on the tray, untouched, the watery scoop of mashed potato hardening around the edges, the sad little chop stony cold.

But, no matter how weak Gran felt, her spirit was eternally buoyant. Her face lit up. 'Hello, dear,' she gasped as Cate bent to kiss her and arrange her pillows to support her. 'How was today? Did you see anything about the memorial?'

Cate beamed. 'You'll never guess who they sent to cover it, Gran.'

As a newspaperwoman herself, Gran understood. Her eyes widened in joyous disbelief. *'No!* Not you?'

Cate nodded, and set about finding a willing staff member to insist the meal be replaced—gently, so they wouldn't take it out on Gran after she'd gone.

When her grandmother was settled and comfortable, Cate pushed aside her anxiety about Tom to give her an edited account of her day's activities. How painful it was, having to strain so carefully any information she gave her now, when Gran had always been the chief confidante of her life.

Before that night. As always when she thought of the scene and its aftermath she struggled with her guilt. The doctors had assured her Gran might have had the heart seizure anyway, even if she and Steve hadn't been arguing across her vulnerable body.

Cate wrung her hands in her lap. She should never have let it happen. She wished she could turn back the clock to the days when Gran had sat over the morning dailies with her specs perched on the end of her nose and a pencil tucked behind her ear.

She sat forward on the steel visitor's chair, managing to describe the service and answer her questions about Tom without making any dangerous revelations. Even so, illness had done nothing to weaken her grandmother's sharp, incisive brain.

Propped up on her pillows, she was studying her, much in the same way Marge had. What was wrong with everyone? Guilt and pity wrung Cate's heart. She hated deceiving her when she was helpless and at the mercy of other people's goodwill.

Though desperately conscious of the clock, Cate couldn't leave her alone among strangers so abruptly. She fought her pricking urgency to fly, and suggested a quick game of Scrabble.

Perhaps Gran sensed her edginess, though, or she was tired, because, to Cate's extreme relief, after ten minutes she lay back on her pillows and shooed her home.

It was close to eight when Cate ran up the stairs to shower and change. The spring evening was warm, far warmer than it should have been for the time of year, so she risked a chiffon evening dress from last summer. It was cut to plunge to her breasts then swirl about her in a bluish-green cloud, with a little triangle of satin and sequins at the cleavage to keep it modest.

She brushed her hair out and let it hang free, applied some deeper eyeshadow and dark red lipstick, threw some things into a suitcase, and, cursing the loss of her mobile, raced down to the pay-phone in the hall to call for a taxi. Luckily, she didn't have to queue.

She was outside on the porch, waiting under the light so the driver could see her, when a car swerved into the driveway and slewed to a halt.

The driver's door opened and a man got out. Her heart sank.

It was Steve.

She'd have filed hours ago, Tom thought. Five at the latest. So where was she? He prowled restlessly to the window. The dark had deepened and the city was coming alive with neon. Security had told him she lived just across the water, at Kirribilli.

She might, just might have been delayed.

The other possibility clawed at his gut. If she'd betrayed him she wouldn't be back. Even now, news of his merger might be in the process of being posted on the *Clarion*'s website, although there was no sign yet of the feeding frenzy this would generate.

He strode into his study and flicked to *Clarion.com*. Not a hint yet. Just the first celebrity pictures from the memorial on their breaking news. Saturday's online edition wouldn't be posted until after midnight.

So where was she? Still at work, frantically digging for back-up to confirm the bombshell she'd filed for tomorrow's daily? Was she capable of such deceit?

How much of a fool had he been to trust that sweet, low voice on the phone? He'd wanted to. God, how he'd wanted to. He felt a momentary regret at having restrained his urge after her flight from the Ferrari to storm into the *Clarion*'s newsroom and grab her by her glorious hair, drag her to the car, and drive her to some secure location. Once she'd given him the slip, it had savaged him when he'd realised he could do nothing but wait and trust in her integrity. Had the phone call been enough to keep the connection alive?

It was so easy for a woman to lie on the phone.

Although, although…

Was there reason to panic? Hadn't there been some quality about her? Hadn't some instinct drawn him to believe in her sincerity?

The image of her rapt face, her lashes fanned against her soft cheeks, swam stirringly into his mind. He felt certain he knew now how she'd look asleep, her hair tumbled on the pillow. His imagination flitted to her rising from the bubbles in his spa like Aphrodite, her satin skin all golden and glistening. If that blonde hair was natural, he mused, it would be blonde all over.

He shook the image off. The strain must be getting to him. All through the strategy meetings with his lawyers and stockbrokers, he'd had to struggle to concentrate. Him, Tom Russell!

He glanced at his watch and saw it was well after eight. Time to cut his losses. The bleak evening stretched before him like a black cavern. With grim resignation he reached for the phone, then paused.

What if she was on her way to him?

It suddenly occurred to him she could be having car trouble. What if she were forced to use public transport? He could imagine her taking an appalling risk of that sort, negotiating the ferry and the city streets alone at night. Even now she might be walking down some shadowy street to the ferry port, her pale hair floating behind her, a flaming invitation to every criminal opportunist, every Tom, Dick and…

He sprang to the hotel phone and ordered Timmins, 'The Merc. *Now*.'

A short time later, conscious of an unusual elevation in his heart-rate, he turned the discreet, dark-tinted sedan into her street. It was one of Kirribilli's wider, busier streets. Boarding houses and small private hotels rose on either side, remnants of a more gracious era when houses had been rambling and fanciful. Some showed signs of recent renovation, with brave new paintwork and solar lights softly illuminating their old

Sydney gardens of rose and hibiscus. Most of them now, though, were the down-at-heel, economical residences shared by students and workers on modest incomes.

There'd been no sign of her at the ferry, or on the footpaths of the narrow undulating streets between her address and the dock. He drove slowly, narrowing his eyes to distinguish the numbers on mail boxes, a buzz in his veins about seeing the place where she lived. He forced himself to take some deep, slow breaths, though it was only natural he should experience a certain interest in seeing her home. He was hardly a stalker, for God's sake.

Halfway along he spotted the number, coming up on his right. He slowed to a halt and let the engine idle. The building was a grand old Victorian villa set back from the road, with a long lawn and extensive garden. It was of several storeys, with balconies beneath its narrow windows haphazardly embellished with iron lace. Even now, with its pleasant shrubbery and the flowery creeper trailing over its well-lit portico, it possessed a turn-of-century charm.

He scanned the lighted windows, his heart quickening. Which of them was hers?

A couple of girls swung out of the iron gate and walked down the street, laughing and chattering. He imagined what life here must be like for Cate Summerfield. She would always have people to talk to, the sorts of easy friendships and entertainments he had himself enjoyed in his university years.

She'd never have known what it was like to grow up behind stone walls, protected and isolated from the real world. He felt a pang of envy for the freedoms people with ordinary lives took for granted. Somehow, her free and easy lifestyle added to her glamour.

Headlights beamed up in his rear vision mirror. When the car had passed by, he drove on until, almost level with the house, he saw a couple standing in the porch.

With a visceral leap he saw that the woman was Cate, and

slammed his foot on the brake. No need to worry she might notice a car stalled across the street. She was too involved in talking to the guy, gazing up at him, listening to him in that heart-stopping way as if she were drinking in his very essence.

Exactly the way she'd looked at *him*.

In the instant he took the scene in, a million thoughts jostled in his brain. It was clear they knew each other well. The guy was inclining his body towards her and gesticulating, while she... Tom recognised that little lift of her chin. It always accompanied some impudent retort. Some sarcastic, clever, maddening, utterly desirable...

He felt his insides clench. The body language was a dead give-away. The guy was hooked on her. Although, hadn't he seen him before? At that instant the man moved directly under the light and Tom caught the flash of red hair.

A savage mix of emotions battled for supremacy in his chest. Anger. A cold, cynical certainty that she was working with the guy, was probably even now spilling everything she'd overheard between himself and Olivia. Fury at his own idiocy in trusting her, and some other darker emotion, to do with smashing the reporter's teeth down his neck until he choked.

He knew what would happen next. The lovers' quarrel would reach a pitch, then explode in passion. The guy would take her in his arms, and in seconds she'd be leading him inside the house... He gripped the wheel. He'd only known her for a day, so why should her betrayal cut so deep? When would he ever learn about women?

Forced to move on, he drove further along until he reached a roundabout near to a small shopping centre, then made a quick U-turn. He cruised back, took one final look to cement her lying, deceiving image into his memory for all time, and abandoned Cate Summerfield to her treachery.

With his usual practice he severed all unwonted emotion and preserved his iron self-control until he kicked the door wide and walked back into the suite. Then something like an extreme weariness came over him. He flicked on the television, but for once in his life he didn't even have the energy to check for the breaking news.

He moved to the window and stared across the water to where the lights of Kirribilli mocked him. First his wife gone, now his father, the last living soul he could truly call his own. Was it any wonder he'd felt attracted by a woman who seemed to effervesce with joyous, carefree life?

She was nothing like Sandra. Sandra had been a serious person. They'd joked about it, but there'd been a nobility in her dedication to her work that he'd sincerely admired. Few people could boast of improving the lot of the human race. But for the first time since her death his avoidance of the delights of feminine company seemed a hollow thing. He made the wry acknowledgement that his self-imposed deprivation hadn't brought her back.

A treacherous thought crept in—would he have even *wanted* her back?—but he exiled it immediately. Of course he would—at least, he'd want the Sandra she'd been when he'd first met her. Before she'd become too involved with her project to leave and follow him home to Oz. Too involved to return his calls, answer his emails. And on that last desperate visit—meet his eyes.

He was a different animal now. A man who lived for his work. Perhaps Marcus had been right to give it all away. Ruthless, but right. If only the old devil could have warned him. Even at the end, on his deathbed, he hadn't said a word. Would the hurt ever ease?

He dragged the letter from his pocket. It was developing tatters, after two weeks of him carrying it about, transferring it from suit to suit of clothes, almost as though he needed to keep it with him for fear of forgetting. He spread it open, and was staring blindly at its grim message when out of nowhere a horror sprang into his mind, something that tore at his gut with such ferocious savagery, it was all he could do to hold in the pain.

The letter. That other devastating letter. The one that had come after Sandra's funeral. From her lover, expressing sincere sympathy for their joint loss.

Thoughts of it had crept up on him before, a million times. But, as if he'd been anaesthetised from it until this moment, the full sickening measure of that betrayal slammed him as if for the first time.

How had he hidden the truth from himself for so long? Why hadn't he realised? Why, in the teeth of all the evidence, had he clung to the myth he'd created about her? He battled with the question of his astounding willingness to accept lies, then his fatigue seemed to settle into his bones.

It occurred to him that even if his conscious mind had avoided the full import, other parts of him must have absorbed it to the full. The truth had seeped like acid down through the layers, through his heart and soul and into his very guts, destroying all the places where love and trust and hope had dwelt, leaving him empty.

All the stresses and strains of sleepless, anxious nights since the bleak little funeral on that green hillside mounted into a black towering wave, poised to crash over him.

For the first time he contemplated letting it all slide. Allowing the corporation to break up, selling off the assets, escaping to somewhere...

It was clear enough what he had to do. He needed to set the wheels in motion. Call his lawyer. Arrange for the press conference.

In the meantime, though, he'd phone down for a bottle of Scotch.

CHAPTER NINE

THE CHATEAU BLEU appeared quiet, its soft lights glimmering. Cate paid off the taxi and hurried through the entrance. Almost at once she was surrounded by uniformed security men. After a brief, heated exchange, in which she had to produce her ID and only just avoided being frisked, Timmins was called to identify her. He flicked a number on his mobile, waited for what seemed like for ever, listened impassively, then snapped the phone shut. Just as he was putting it away it rang. This time, after another interminable conversation, during which he kept turning to look at her muttering things she couldn't hear, she was allowed to pass.

Upstairs she put her bag down outside Tom's door, wondering if she'd need it, conscious of the sudden violence of her heartbeat. She wiped nervous hands on her skirt, felt her mouth go dry. What if he'd carried out his threat and called off his merger? How furious was he likely to be? She'd been through enough for one night, with Steve trying to talk his way back in.

She raised her fist to knock, but before she could make contact the door opened. Tom Russell stood there, frowning and looking vaguely dishevelled. From somewhere in the background came the deep sombre strains of a cello. He stood staring at her with a strange light in his eyes, and there was an electric, insane instant when she was actually tempted to rush into his arms, but thank God inhibition held her back.

'Ah,' he said, blinking his black lashes. 'My girlfriend.' She was disconcerted to see a fiery little glow in the depths of his eyes, as if he were fuelled up on something. Anger?

'I'm sorry I was delayed, Tom. Honestly.' She was so afraid of the answer she hardly dared ask. 'Is it—am I too late?'

He had a slightly rakish appearance. His five o'clock shadow was strongly in evidence, and, although he'd changed into the sort of well-cut casual trousers and shirt any billionaire about town might wear, say on a date with—in his case—an aeronautic physicist, his clothes were a little crushed. The shirt hung loose, its sleeves rolled back to reveal his sinewy forearms.

She noticed too that his hair was mussed, with a tendency to fall forward on his forehead, as if someone should smooth it back for him. He might have been any guy having a relaxed evening at home. Any thrilling guy, that was, with a body to make a woman's knees go weak and billions flowing down the drain because she was late.

The suspense was killing her. She met his gaze, her adrenaline building. 'Well? Did you call off your merger?'

Merger? Tom wondered. He leaned against the door jamb and stared at her eager, anxious face through a mild alcoholic haze. Maybe he was drunker than he thought, but the news of her arrival had rocked his grim doubts off their foundations and illuminated his heart like a solar burst.

He dragged a hand through his hair to give the new reality time to align itself. She was here. She'd never have come back if she'd betrayed him.

He'd been wrong.

His heavy spirits caught an up draught of light, clean air and soared straight up through the stratosphere.

It seemed incredible now to think of how he'd doubted her. Surely those clear, luminous eyes were incapable of concealment. Seeing her again in the flesh, in her glorious, womanly flesh...

He tried not to stare at her breasts, but that little glittery triangle drew his eyes to the gorgeous swells like magnets. His hands itched with the need to feel their soft resilience. For some reason, the satin inset only made his mind jump to another triangle, the forbidden one hidden tantalisingly under her clothes.

He felt his loins stir and forced himself to concentrate on her face.

That was hardly easier. Tonight her eyes were of the deepest aquamarine, in echo of the dress. Her lashes seemed longer, her lips a richer ruby-red. His own lips yearned with the memory of their yielding sweetness. He wanted to plunge his tongue into that moist, wine-sweet cavern and fill up his senses with the taste of her.

He no sooner imagined that voluptuous possibility than, with that amazing synchronicity, almost like some sort of thought transference, he saw her pupils dilate. At once he knew with a gut-deep, primeval certainty his instincts were right. She could feel the pull as irresistibly as he could. Suddenly he felt as sure and smooth as top-class tyres on a new-laid road.

When he spoke his voice came out deeper than a cave-dweller's. 'You're late.'

Cate, prepared for the worst, felt her insides clench. 'I know. As I said, I was delayed. You didn't—you didn't call off your merger, did you?'

She tried to read his expression as he surveyed every inch of her from beneath heavy brows.

'That's quite a pretty dress,' he growled. 'It looks as if you're going somewhere.' Then he smiled. Such a sexy smile.

Sweet, joyous relief flooded through her. This wasn't the response of an angry man. And a sensual little quirk stayed in one corner of his mouth, as if he just might be pleased to see her.

Boosted by the flirty signals, her nerve bounced back. 'Well, I am. Here.' She pointed to the floor. 'Though God knows why,' she added, rolling her eyes.

'We both know why.' He took the bag from her and pulled her inside. 'So what kept you?' he demanded. 'What could possibly have been more important than your deal with me?'

Despite the severity of his tone he found a strand of her hair that needed smoothing from her face, and her ear tingled in shameless pleasure. She probably wouldn't have resisted if he'd started stroking her neck.

'Well, in case you've forgotten, I had a story to file. I was delayed getting back to the newsroom...*remember*?' She glowered at him. 'I was running so late I missed my train... I was late for my grandmother... I had to wait absolutely ages for a cab...Do you have any idea what Sydney's like for mere mortals on a Friday night? Not everyone gets driven about in limos, you know.'

'Still very passionate, I see.'

Passionate? She looked narrowly at him. This was hardly the sort of word tossed about lightly by a sophisticated beast she was moving in with for the night. That hot spark lurking in his eyes was unsettling, but he seemed steady and controlled, his speech as crisp as ever. Or was it?

'So what else happened to delay you?' he said. 'What other insurmountable obstacles stood between you and your lover?'

He'd managed 'insurmountable' and 'obstacles' very well. Almost too well. As if he'd taken care not to allow any blurring around the edges of the words. And then there were the words themselves.

Examining him minutely, she said, 'You mean apart from the hot coals and the swim across the harbour? Wasn't that enough?' She smiled at him. 'Anyway, I was afraid you'd think I'd ratted.'

She started to move down the hall, and when he didn't immediately follow, flashed a glance back at him. He was watching her with a small frown, and she felt a sudden anxious lurch. 'You didn't—you didn't throw in the towel on your merger, Tom, did you?'

To her intense relief his expression and the posture of his big, lean frame relaxed. 'Never,' he scoffed, waving his hand. 'Why would I do that? I knew you'd be here.' He caught up to her, a touch of swagger in his step. He slipped an arm around her waist and murmured into her ear, making it tickle. 'I knew you wouldn't be able to resist.'

'Why wouldn't I?' she retorted, smiling, though the giddy blood rushed up to her neck. 'Because you're so irresistible?'

'Well, you haven't resisted very hard so far, have you?' He broke into a grin that was pure, sinful sex.

There was whisky on his breath, and a recklessness in his smile that charmed her to her entrails. This cocksure cowboy was a million miles from the icy, driven despot who'd thrilled and threatened her in the cathedral.

He swept her with him into the dimly lit sitting room and left her there while he went to deposit her bag.

She looked around her with a small shock. She had been aware from the first of the austere music leaking through the front door. Now she noticed that the apartment had an atmosphere of desolation, perhaps because the blinds were all open and darkness, punctuated by the hard glitter of the city lights, pressed against the glass. Apart from the bright foyer, the lighting inside the rooms relied on a single lamp on a sofa table in the sitting room, combined with a weak glow issuing from the kitchen.

A plasma screen flickered soundlessly across from a sofa. Had Tom been watching the news channel in the dark— endless silent images of misery and disaster? She bit her lip. The sense she'd had at the memorial service of his tightly controlled restraint returned with greater force.

For some reason the memory floated into her mind of the waste-paper bin she'd seen, crammed with the clothes he'd worn at the memorial. At the time she'd been shocked by the sheer wanton waste. Now she realised there was a deeper significance to his disposal of them. Why hadn't she understood?

It seemed obvious now that his clothes must have felt tainted by the occasion.

She turned when she heard his step behind her.

'Is there some guy breaking his heart over you tonight, Goldilocks?' Though his tone was casual, his eyes were alert.

Startled, she thought of Steve, attempting yet again to reopen the lines of communication, then she shrugged and grinned. 'There may be one or two who'd like to murder me. Can you imagine?' She fluttered her lashes.

He reached out and traced his long, lean fingers from her eyebrow to her jaw. 'They're all too late,' he said softly. 'I get first refusal on murdering you.'

His voice was as caressing as his lazy, sensual touch, and scorched a shivery yearning path through her interior.

He inclined his head, grazing her cheek with his as he closed his eyes to inhale her perfume. 'Ah-h-h…sexy.' Then just as she anticipated his kiss he released her, leaving her breathless and aroused. His careless, light-hearted mood was irresistible, but she wasn't sure she could believe in it. Not here in the semi-dark, with music to wring the soul.

Did Tom Russell's easy laugh conceal deep, unsheddable tears? He was such a strong, assured man the idea needed getting used to, although Gran always said sons could suffer badly from the death of a father. And she'd read often enough that men weren't as well equipped for the release of grief as women.

She indicated the television monitor. 'Were you watching something?'

He shrugged. 'Just keeping my eye on the news. To see what breaks.'

To learn if she'd broken the story, she guessed with growing dismay at her part in his distress, watching him pick up a remote control and click the television off. To find out if she'd betrayed him.

Her eye fell on a whisky bottle and glass standing on the coffee table in front of the sofa. The liquid level in the bottle was at about the three-quarter mark. She looked around again at the dimly lit rooms, the stark windows open to the night, and felt moved. This was no scene of celebration. More like a wake. Had he had any food this day? she wondered.

She felt the heat of his gaze scorch her bare arms and legs. Awareness warmed her, and as though he'd read the tremor in her blood his mouth edged up a little at the corners. She remembered well how those lips had tasted. How she'd burned.

'That really is a pretty dress, Cate.' Seduction gleamed in his eyes. 'Why don't you take it off?'

She looked wonderingly at him. 'Are you drunk, Tom?'

'Not yet.' He dropped onto the sofa and stretched out his long legs, lifting one negligent foot onto the coffee table. In the glow of the lamp he looked more relaxed than she'd seen him all day. He patted the spot next to him in smiling invitation, wickedness in his eyes. 'Why don't you sit down?'

She could feel herself sliding. Alcohol had done nothing to diminish his attraction. That bad-boy charm combined with his lean, dark sexiness was enough to tempt a saint, let alone Cate Summerfield. It had been a long time since a desirable man had eaten her up with his eyes.

But there were questions she needed settled. Like where she was to sleep. She'd only seen the one bed, earlier. In the current mood it seemed doubtful he'd have organised anything for her. She needed to know what he had in mind.

The cello wound its poignant song to an end. In the sudden stillness she could hear her own nervy heartbeat.

'Er…Tom. Where do you want me to sleep?' Try as she might, there was no concealing the husky awareness in her voice.

He hesitated, the gleam in his eyes piercingly sensual. The silence deepened and grew electric.

Desire rustled in the breeze from the balcony, whispered in her hair, burned in the gaze flickering from her bare arms to her legs, her mouth, her throat and breasts. Her heart skittered into double time. Was this the game she'd come to play? Tempting though it was, how wise would it be to get in deep with Tom Russell? He was no callow boy. Would she be able to manage a quick and easy exit?

He walked across to her and gripped her arms. The seriousness of his lean, strong face startled her. Sincerity rang like steel in his voice, harshened the lines from cheek to jaw, reminding her of the pitfalls of playing with fire.

'Why did you come back? You know you could have ruined me.' He searched her face and his voice deepened. 'Are you really what you seem?'

His intensity trapped her breath and stirred her feminine being at the most primitive level. Her reasons for returning swam confusedly in her mind. She'd kept her part of the bargain. That was why she'd come back, wasn't it?

'You know why,' she faltered. 'I promised. And you said on the phone…'

'What did I say?' He cupped her face, brushed her mouth sexily with his lips. 'Did I tell you I want you?'

He pushed her, unresisting, against the wall, holding her there while he trailed an exploratory finger from her cheek, down her throat to trace her collar bone. His hand slipped under the satin at her cleavage, his light touch sending shivers of pleasure through her as he traced the swell into her bra. He cupped her breast in his warm palm while her blood thundered in her ears.

Against the room's muted glow his harsh outline was set in relief from cheekbone to sculpted jaw. Though the available light was low, she could see the flex of sinews in his strong neck, see his eyelids grow heavy with sensuality as he caressed her willing breasts with his smooth, lean fingers.

The power radiating from him dragged at her breathing. Heavy heat unfurled deep in her insides and swelled her nipples, igniting her erotic places with a fierce yearning ache.

He was beautiful, she thought, quivering as spears of flame

shot through her flesh wherever he touched. Beautiful and dangerous.

He slipped a hand under the hair at her nape. 'That kiss today,' he murmured, his voice dark and sultry. 'I'm not sure it was the best we can do.'

She contemplated his mouth. 'I knew I could have done better,' she breathed, 'but I didn't want to take a slutty advantage of you.'

He brought his lips down on hers, and it was no tepid kiss. It was a searing demand, his lips confident and assured after the kisses earlier in the day. Her senses surged to the feel and scent and taste of him, familiar to her now. The added tincture of whisky escalated the element of risk, accelerated her excitement.

He tasted each of her lips with such thrilling sensual artistry, her bones turned to liquid and she had to cling to his wide shoulders to support herself. An instant before her brain dissolved in the mists of passion, the thought flashed through her mind... What if she couldn't control this?

But, aroused, she gave herself up to the sizzling delights. Impressively, the whisky hadn't dulled his skills. While he seduced her mouth with his lips and tongue with exquisite care, his urgent hands plundered her body with inspired ruthlessness. He made wicked forays under her dress to explore her hips and thighs and stroke her bottom, invoking delicious trails of flame, heightening her fever for more.

Wherever he touched her, fire raged. In her lips, in the tissues inside her mouth, in her tender, swollen breasts. It licked along her veins, and inflamed wild cravings between her legs.

He broke from her lips to deliver hot greedy kisses down her throat to her breasts. Painfully aroused, her nipples strained for his touch. As though in instinctive understanding, he sucked the yearning peaks one after the other through the fabrics of her dress and bra.

His touch was so subtle and erotic, it was like paraffin to

the flame. Desire blazed in her blood, arousing such a desperate hunger she felt a rush of moisture in her pants.

In a frenzy for deeper, more intimate contact, she writhed in his strong arms, exulting in the hard length of his erection prodding her belly, lusting to feel the hot rod stroking her where it counted. To dare him on she pushed up his shirt, exploring in the dark with avid hands his smooth, satin skin, the gorgeous contours of his pectorals and hard, flat abdominal muscles.

The strong rhythm of his heart beat against her ear, moving in its great invincible power, while at the same time so human and vulnerable. Somehow the thought of that intensified her passion for him. With thirsty lips she tasted his hot, salty skin and felt his chest hairs graze her cheek. Unbearably tantalised, knowing she was raising the stakes, she licked one of his nipples.

A satisfying shudder rippled through his big frame. Groaning her name, he sank to his knees, his arms around her hips, and pressed his mouth hungrily into her dress at the juncture of her thighs.

The shock sent a deep gasp of excitement through her, and she sagged, trembling, against the wall, barely able to support herself, while, through the thin layers of her clothing, he invaded the secrets of her mound with his sexy mouth.

It was thrilling, it was titillating, it felt rapturously good. She panted for the delicious pleasure to go on and on, to get deeper, closer, wilder, and when he lifted her dress over his head and licked seductively across the flimsy fabric of her pants, she hardly recognised the hoarse animal sound that came from her own throat. She leaned back against the wall, her legs parted for him, willing the forbidden ecstasy to continue, quivering when his cunning tongue tip strayed inside the fabric and flicked across her most intimate place.

She was interrupted from her swooning pleasure by a gradual and increasing awareness of hammering. At almost the same time, Tom Russell drew abruptly apart from her, causing her to overbalance and sprawl gracelessly on top of him.

She heard him yelp with pain, and curse. He shifted position to prevent her knee from crushing his most vulnerable asset and her elbow from piercing his neck. After a stunned second, she scrambled up, feeling herself go scarlet with embarrassment. He followed suit more slowly, groaning at first, then breaking into a laugh.

Hot and discomfited as she was, that laugh stung like fury. Did the man have a sensitive bone in his body?

It impinged on her foggy brain that the hammering was someone knocking at the front door. She made a panicked attempt to smooth her hair and dress and cool her face with her fingers, ignoring Tom as he turned away from her to make adjustments to his clothes.

It reminded her only too rawly of the aftermath of the fateful kiss at the yacht club. This time, though, her mortification was made worse by the awkward and painful discomfort of unresolved lust. And would he blame her, this time?

She felt him glance her way again and avoided his eyes.

'That'll be dinner,' he said, his voice like a gravel pit. At least he'd stopped laughing. He stood for a few pregnant seconds pushing back his hair, then after some strained moments in which neither of them uttered a word, made for the door.

She heard the murmur of voices, and, casting about for a bolt hole, shrank through the nearest doorway and into the blessed shadows of his bedroom.

The shadows were short-lived. Tom must have finally noticed the gloom and flicked a switch, because lights snapped on all over the apartment. Standing just inside the open bedroom door, she was caught, petrified, in the spotlight as a crowd of kitchen staff passed by and all turned to stare at her.

On the one hand she should have been pleased. If a procession of chefs and waiters, the first wheeling a table set for two, countless others bearing stainless-steel chafing dishes, all supervised by a grandiose butler with a supercilious expression, *had* to enter a scene of unbridled lust, it was probably better if they didn't find the place suspiciously dark.

On the other hand, a woman who had just been kissed to within an inch of her life naturally felt cautious about advertising the fact. Hoping the passing parade hadn't had enough time to properly register her, she summoned the strength to push the door to, and tottered to the bathroom, closing the door firmly behind her.

At first she had to blink, dazzled by the light. A blaze of white and gold marble bounced from miles of faceted mirrors, until her eyes accustomed and she saw the mirrors had been cunningly placed to give never-ending reflections. She noted a shower cubicle large enough to host a reception, a deep luxurious spa bath with gold tap-fittings, and an elegant toilet and bidet in sparkling fluted porcelain, the like of which had never graced the boarding house. But it was her appearance she was most concerned about.

She looked a mess.

Her bodice was slightly askew, her hair ruined. Worse was her face. Her eyes looked languorous and overbright, her mouth as swollen as a Hollywood starlet's. There were red blotches on her throat and chest, damning evidence of Tom's enthusiasm.

How could she have participated in something so shocking?

She closed her eyes. Shocking but fantastic.

Just remembering the intensity of the onslaught threatened to melt her insides, and she had to breathe deeply until the storm passed.

She cast about for something she could use for repairs. Surprisingly, feminine toiletries had been placed on the wide vanity, including high quality shampoo and conditioner she would never have afforded for herself, fragrant gels and body washes, bath salts in lavender and honeysuckle, stored in pretty bottles.

She washed, then dried herself on one of several fluffy

white towels folded on a rack. Without the benefit of make-up, she had to resort to patting some talc onto her throat, and smoothed liberal quantities of moisturiser onto her mouth. She ran an experimental finger over her lips. There wasn't much more she could do without some proper lipsalve. Satisfied, though, that she looked at least semi-human, she opened the door, hoping the kitchen crew would have left by now, and ventured back into Tom's bedroom.

It was the first time she'd really had a chance to appreciate it. Its furnishings were sparse and somehow masculine, with pure lines and uncompromising edges. The polished floorboards were bare, apart from a glistening silken rug some fine oriental hand had woven with the Tree of Life. Nightingales, hummingbirds and peacocks fluttered through its gorgeous branches.

Heavy silk curtains half obscured the view. On another wall a small exquisite watercolour showed the harbour from almost the same vantage point over a hundred years earlier. She moved closer to peer at its lower right hand corner and saw it was a Streeton. And it was real. Of course it was.

And there was the bed. For a second she allowed herself to take in its full voluptuous extent, with its quilt turned down, the lamplight warming its pillows. The sexual prospects of that seductive bed swam before her eyes, and her insides warmed and coiled in a confused mingling of sensations.

It was then she noticed her overnight bag, reposing on a bench created for that purpose. Tom must have placed it there as soon as she'd arrived. She frowned, realising that that had been before they'd even kissed. With dismay it occurred to her that he'd just taken it for granted she would sleep with him. Certainly a woman expected invitations, but this—

Discomfort gnawed at her. It was one thing to be attracted to someone, even to engage in a little flirtation, quite another for that attraction to translate into sex. Nothing could have shown more clearly what he thought of her. What had she done to convince him of her easy compliance?

Although, it wasn't as if she cared what he thought of her, was it?

Except… Something panged in her chest. It was no use telling herself she didn't care what he thought. Ridiculous, but she did. And if she challenged him about it now, after engaging in that sizzling hot clinch, she'd have no credibility. The only thing left to her to retrieve her pride was to make sure he understood she wouldn't sleep with him under any circumstances. There would be no more kissing, no more… Dismay at her wanton behaviour crept through her and she covered her cheeks with her hands.

Face it. She'd only known him a day. Could she have lost all touch with reality? She'd *known* he'd had too much to drink, the circumstances weren't exactly romantic, only a few hours earlier he'd been treating her with dislike. He knew nothing whatsoever about her, or her life. He didn't have the slightest interest in her as a person. She would have to… Damn, if she was to live with herself she'd have to deal with it. Straighten it out with him. Tell him plainly where she stood. Otherwise…well, perhaps she'd have to consider leaving.

Hopeful that the staff had gone, she opened the bedroom door a crack. Clattering sounds came from the kitchen, and savoury aromas that sent her weak at the knees. Her poor stomach rumbled. If she had to leave, surely she could wait until after dinner?

Steeling herself for public exposure, she drew a deep breath and walked out into the sitting room. Voices came from the kitchen, and she noticed that the balcony was now a blaze of light. A waiter was out there hovering over the table.

Tom materialised from the kitchen holding two glasses of champagne, and her stern resolutions fell, panting, to their knees. His smile was so darkly wicked and sinful, as if there was some bad conspiracy between them. And there was. Her weak, treacherous body knew it only too well. He pressed a glass into her hand, appraising her with a veiled, solemn look. 'Are you—all right?'

'Of course I'm all right,' she snapped.

What did he think—that she was too unsophisticated to move on from a minor embarrassment? At once she was transported back to that frantic moment when she parted her legs so he could plunder her with his mouth. Against her will, she couldn't repress the hot sensual tide that rose at ankle level and flooded her all the way up through her neck to the roots of her hair.

Anger with him for having such inflammatory power over her when she was struggling for poise made her terser with him than she might otherwise have been.

Anyway, with that predatory alcoholic glow in his eyes, should he even be drinking champagne?

'I see you've put my suitcase in your room,' she asserted coldly.

His brows made an amused twitch. 'It seemed the best place.'

'Why is that?'

'Well, the bed is comfortable, and I thought you'd enjoy the bathroom. The spa in there is—quite good.' His black lashes flickered sensuously down.

'Is it? And where do you think you'll be sleeping?'

He scratched his ear. After the briefest hesitation, he said, 'Ah…well. Along here. Come, I'll show you.' He held out his hand to take hers but she coolly avoided it.

She accompanied him along the small hallway that led past the kitchen, where a small crowd was now busily ensconced, and showed her into his study.

Her jaw dropped. To her complete surprise she saw that a bed had been set up in there. After a few nonplussed seconds, in which she tried to look as nonchalant as if she'd expected it all along, she followed him inside.

The room was a gracious and pleasant-sized second bedroom. Its walls were lined with bookshelves from ceiling to floor, much like Gran's, only on a grander scale. There was an *en suite* bathroom she hadn't noticed at her earlier visit, showing signs of masculine occupation. Although its fittings were similar to the one in the master suite, it was smaller and not equipped with a spa.

'I work in here at night,' he explained, leaning his tall frame against his desk and ravishing her with smiling, heavy-lidded eyes. 'I wouldn't like to think I was disturbing your sleep.'

'Oh.' She felt her flush rise again, and turned sharply away to conceal it. It should have been a relief to be able to exonerate him, but somehow it made things more complicated than ever. Everything felt wrong. Posh penthouses with their Persian rugs and gold-fitted marble only irritated her. And how...*how* could a woman talk to a man she barely knew...after...?

'It's—it's very good of you to give up your room. Are you sure you want to do that? I'm sorry if I seemed...I didn't want to think you might have made some assumption...'

His eyes were glinting in that way that made it hard to know if he was being sincere, or subtly mocking her and dying to laugh. 'No need to apologise. If you think about it, it would look strange if you weren't sleeping in my bed. It would certainly arouse the suspicions of the staff. And then if anyone were to drop by...'

'Oh, you mean...Malcolm Devlin?' He hesitated to reply, and she added, trying to read his expression, 'You did say he was coming tonight. Isn't that why it was so urgent for me to—be here?'

His eyes shimmered, and a small prickling silence fell. 'One of the reasons,' he said at last. 'As a matter of fact, I— put him off.'

He didn't smile. His stirringly sensuous mouth was grave, but she had a sudden piercing insight. Malcolm Devlin wasn't coming. He'd never been coming. And she knew without a doubt that Tom Russell was as aware as she was of the question clammering in her head and pulsing between them like an electric current.

She tried to bury its insidious little voice and consign it to the outer regions of hell, but it *would* come back and insist on asking itself.

If, it shrilled in her frontal lobes, a man and a woman had engaged in an activity that had failed to reach its natural conclusion, what happened then?

CHAPTER TEN

DINNER on the balcony had a certain ambience. From her chair Cate could see the harbour lights, the streaming blaze of headlights overhead on the great bridge, and, rising tier upon tier from all around the shoreline, millions of glowing golden dots that were people's private windows.

It was magic. It gave Sydney a cosy, intimate feel, as if personal communications were bouncing from shore to shore across the harbour, and she and Tom were part of them.

The fairyland effect was enhanced by the excellence of the food. It convinced her that a billionaire employing a private chef didn't have to be a social evil.

A chef needed a job, after all. And when Tom introduced her to his chef, his butler, and the waiter with friendly humour, as people he valued and respected, she found it hard not to see him through their eyes. Certainly, he was their boss. She was pretty sure he'd be exacting, even impatient. But she could see they liked and respected him, and weren't too in awe of him to crack a joke.

If Gran could have seen her now. Actually, she was glad Gran couldn't. So much would be hard to explain. And she knew what the people in the newsroom would say. They'd accuse her of selling out her principles to big business interests.

'Does your butler always serve you dinner out here?'

Tom Russell's mouth quivered in amusement. 'I don't often

eat in the apartment. Tonight they thought it was special. They wanted to impress you.'

Soon afterwards, the subtle delicacies of asparagus soup and gnocchi with truffled mushroom sauce washed down with wine eased some of her tensions. Then coral trout flown in from the Great Barrier Reef, and served with fried potatoes and a lime-and-honey-dressed salad, slid down into her grateful interior and quelled the rest of her qualms. She began to forgive Tom for the kiss debacle. A woman had to eat, after all.

Although he'd had a few drinks, Tom's lean, tanned hands moved with the same swift grace as ever, and the only hint of his high-flying mood were the shocking, irreverent stories he told her of celebrities who'd been at the service. She felt that he'd let down his guard to her. He made her laugh and kept her imagination on the simmer, her spine tingling like a thrill-seeker on a fun-park ride. Was this how it would feel to be close to him, like a real girlfriend? What dangerous excitement might he plunge her into next?

Why not admit it? She was hooked on the adrenaline.

By the time the dessert came, though, his mood grew more pensive, as if laughter was becoming too much of an effort to sustain. She sensed the fragility of his emotions, although he still seemed determined to keep serious issues at bay, and concentrated all his energy into finding out about her. He asked her searching questions. Grilled her, in fact, about her friends at work. At one stage when she was relating an amusing anecdote about the newsroom, he interrupted her with, 'Who was the guy you were engaged to? One of your workmates?'

When she hesitated, he said, 'Was it Steve Wilson?'

She raised her brows in surprise. 'How did you know?'

He made a vague, noncommittal gesture then. Later on in the meal, he brought the subject up again. 'So—what went wrong?'

Glancing up, she met his veiled gaze. She shrugged and plunged her spoon into her raspberry and chocolate mousse tart. 'Let's just say he made a mistake.'

His brows shot up. 'Only one?'

She lowered her lashes and slid the spoon into her mouth. 'Mmm.' She closed her eyes to savour the rich, smooth lusciousness.

When she opened them he was watching her with an intense, wolfish hunger. His hot gaze drifted to her throat and breasts. Her thrumming heart began to bump against her ribs. He was thinking about something else, she felt sure. The something that drummed on the breeze like the call of the wild.

Eventually, the remains of the sumptuous tart were cleared away, and he suggested they take their coffee and the dregs of the claret to the sitting room. 'Where we can talk,' he said.

They were drawn to the same sofa he'd occupied earlier. This time Tom replaced the cello suites with a bluesy Miles Davis trumpet recording of 'Summertime.' There was no reason not to relax and engage in some intelligent conversation. So why, all at once, had her speech dried up?

Tom Russell gazed broodingly down at the rich red and blue oriental rug, while the delicate subject loomed silently between them, then he raised his eyes to hers. 'I'm sorry about before, Cate. I do apologise. Very bad timing.' He shook his head. 'Bloody criminal.'

She nodded in stiff acceptance. 'That's—all right. It should never have happened.'

'It certainly shouldn't have.'

'It wasn't part of our agreement. '

'I know. I was a bastard, kissing you like that.'

She glanced quickly at him. His expression was solemn, but she wasn't sure she could trust his sincerity, especially with that sensual glow in his eyes.

He lounged carelessly back against the sofa, and heaved a sigh. 'You know, I think we got off to a bad start this morning.' He stretched his arm along the sofa back. It was an intimate move, and brought him closer. His mouth was relaxed, his warm gaze intent on her face. 'I know I may have seemed—abrupt. I am sorry.'

Her heart swelled with gratitude that he cared enough to apologise. Less than an arm's length away from him, she felt infused with a dangerous tingling warmth, like a small feminine moon sucked irresistibly towards a strong, hot sun.

'I think I understand, Tom. You've been under stress, what with everything. Losing your dad, and all.' She lowered her eyes. 'And look…er…I'm sorry if I hurt you. With the things I wrote about him.'

Unconsciously, her fingers slid down the stem of her glass. She felt his gaze flick to them beneath his black lashes.

He gave a small sardonic laugh. 'Don't apologise. He'd be the first to agree he deserved every word.'

'You must have been very close.'

He made a wry grimace. 'I'd thought so, finally. Although not so much when I was young. He was already in his fifties when I was born, you know. It wasn't until I reached my twenties that we really began to understand each other. At least…I thought we did. I thought we were close. But then, right at the end, he…'

The lean, bronzed fingers tightened on his glass, and he dropped his gaze and lapsed into a brooding silence. The humour lines around his mouth and eyes seemed to deepen and grow pained.

What had happened at the end? Had that old man turned away from his son? She wished she were close enough to him to ask. For a moment he looked so weary her heart ached for him.

'You look so sad,' she exclaimed involuntarily.

At once the shutters came down. His brows snapped together and his guarded gaze set her at bay like an intruder. She could have bitten off her tongue. The last thing Tom Russell wanted from her was sympathy. How inept of her to have trampled on his private feelings. She curled her hands in her lap. How insensitive he must have thought her.

She felt his keen glance on her face. As if he'd read her dismay, he swiftly moved to recover the mood, and gave an easy laugh.

'Sad? Never.' He waved his glass. 'Don't forget the real funeral was more than two weeks ago. It's not as if I haven't been anticipating his end for a long time.' A darker edge crept into his voice. 'It's different when a death comes—suddenly. Then you can feel—knocked about.' He stared, frowning, into his wine, then took a swallow and relapsed back into abstraction.

She remembered that his wife had died suddenly. Hadn't two years been enough to soften the loss? Perhaps not, considering the sharp rebuke he'd given Olivia in the cathedral. The silence lengthened, and she wasn't sure if it was a trick of the lamplight, but a harsh fierceness showed in his strong face, as if he were locked in battle with some private anguish. Her heart swelled with compassion. Despite his light words of denial, the signs of grieving were all there.

She wished she had the right to take him in her arms and offer him solace, and wondered who else there was in his life to help him bear his grief. Surely he should have spent this night in the company of loved ones. If anything happened to Gran, she knew she'd want someone to comfort her through the rugged night watches.

'Sometimes it can catch up on you later,' she observed huskily, needing to break the silence. 'My parents were killed when I was five, then when I was nine I shut down for half a year.'

He roused himself from his musings. '*Both* your parents? Oh, Goldilocks,' he exclaimed softly, reaching out to touch her cheek. After a while he added, 'What does that mean, shut down?'

'I stopped wanting to go to school. In the mornings I stayed in bed and turned my face to the wall. *Me.* Don't laugh, but I lost interest in everything. My friends, games, all the kids' parties. It seems incredible now.'

He considered her for a while, then lightly brushed her hand. 'I'm not laughing. So what did they do to you? Send round the Feds?'

'Well, Gran talked to people at the school and I was allowed some time away. She had to take time off from her job at the paper, and I did my lessons with her. From what I remember, I must have been like a sleepwalker. For months I hardly did anything but practise my violin. I think the music must have helped.'

'What snapped you out of it?'

She smiled. 'Luckily—especially for the music lovers of the neighbourhood—Gran understood what was wrong, and she just waited until I was ready to talk about it. Then one day some friends who'd known Mum and Dad came to visit, and brought up some stories about them from the past. After they'd gone, somehow the floodgates opened.'

She laughed in ridicule of herself, but her eyes still misted over with the glimpse of the old tragedy.

He sat very still, his eyes intent on her face. She could feel him analysing, searching inside her brain with his sharp intelligence. After a while he sighed and frowned down at the rug, then with an impatient gesture tossed off the last of his wine.

'Let's not dwell on it all now. They've gone, all of them. Ashes to ashes.' He turned his slumbrous gaze to her. 'But we're here. *You're* here. And you're so very—very alive.' He reached out and lightly traced her jawbone with his thumb, then his hand slid to her throat. 'I can feel your blood pulsing just here.'

How could a careless touch be so intensely sensual? All at once her blood wasn't blood, and it wasn't merely pulsing. It was wine, and the scorching, high-voltage desire in his eyes sent it seething madly through every vein in her body. More than ever their brief, wild slide into passion before dinner simmered between them like a tangible force. Was this the consolation Tom Russell sought?

She tried to weigh up the issues, the potential conse-
quences, but his magnetic presence only a few centimetres
away sparked fire along her nerves and made her limbs feel
heavy and languorous.

A tiny voice tried to warn her it could be spurious, this
sudden gentleness and accessibility, nothing to do with her at
all. Even macho men had their softer moments. Wouldn't he
be as desirous of any other woman who happened to be here
with him this night?

But there was no other woman. *She* was here, and, trans-
fixed with a longing to be close to him, she couldn't have run
away from him now to save her life. And who else did he
have? she argued with herself.

'Have you—do you have much to do with your stepsisters?'

Amusement crept into his eyes. 'As little as possible.
They're far too keen to hustle me to the altar. They've tried
to set me up with every little diamond-miner in Sydney.'

'That's a pity. I know if Gran died... Well, when it does
eventually happen, a long, long time in the future, touch
wood...I hope I won't be alone to deal with it.'

'She means a lot to you.'

It was a statement more than a question. She nodded, and
his eyes held such warmth and understanding she was seized
by a deep, instinctive certainty. Caught up as he was with his
grief, he still had heart enough to spare for her concerns.
Whatever crazy fate had decreed she should be with him this
night, it felt right.

The fiery glow in his eyes intensified, and he said softly,
'We're neither of us alone tonight, are we?'

Everything in her slowed and held its breath, poised on a
pivot of desire. When Tom Russell put his hand out and gently
tilted up her face, she surrendered to his firm, warm lips with
willing fervour. This time he kissed her with such a slow and
exquisite tenderness her bones melted into liquid fire.

He drew away from her, his breathing a little ragged. His

deep voice thickened. 'If you were my girlfriend now I'd carry you into that bedroom.'

'Well, then,' she breathed over her tumultuous heartbeat, 'let's pretend I'm your girlfriend.'

He put one arm around her, the other under her knees and hoisted her up, laughing as he swayed precariously backwards and forwards, threatening to spill her. She giggled, then cried out with alarm as he nearly overbalanced. Then he changed his grip, and she clasped her arms around his strong neck while he carried her into his bedroom as easily as if she were a leaf.

For a suspenseful moment he stood by the bed, holding her as if preparing to toss her into the middle. He was smiling down at her, devilment in his eyes, then they darkened and his smile faded. He set her down on the rug.

He surveyed her and the air prickled with suspense, as if something between them had reached a critical point. She had a sense of fathomless depths in Tom Russell, of the jagged darkness beneath his lean, sexy surface.

Adrenaline lurched in her belly. Hadn't some part of her known from the very first—the first glance, the first words— that everything this day would lead to this moment? Although how much of his desire was attraction, and how much of it was pain?

He stood before her, straight and tall and silent, sophisticated and sexual, his hot eyes focused on *her*, and she felt an inner surge of sheer exhilaration. She was a woman and she wanted him. There was only now. This one night.

Gently, he lifted the hair from her neck and weighed it in his hand. Immediately her spine became a river of shivers. She could hear his quickened breathing as his smooth fingers sought her zip and found it. She stood very still, her breath coming faster as he slipped the zip down, his gaze intent on her face. As the cool air touched her skin she quivered uncontrollably.

He bent his dark head and her blood leaped in intoxicated

response as her nostrils filled with his clean masculine scent. He kissed the curve of her neck and shoulder, and where his lips touched her skin burned. With a quick movement he slid the dress from her shoulders and it fell to the floor.

His lustful gaze on her near-nakedness fuelled a warm erotic rush to her nipples, and kindled the fire between her legs. He'd hardly touched her, yet her body remembered how aroused she'd been earlier and ignited again, her flesh pricking with desire. Her skin craved the caresses of those smooth, lean hands, his artful, sensuous mouth.

To speed things along she reached for his shirt, but he caught her hands and held them still.

'Not yet,' he growled, his deep voice reaching into her with its dark authority, stirring her longings to be with him, to draw closer to him.

He unfastened her lacy bra with hands that were only just steady. Panting, she helped him, her own eager hands trembling. His eyes flared at the sight of her bare breasts, the nipples taut and ripe, and though her longing for him to touch them, *taste* them, roared, he knelt down. Caressingly, as if she were of priceless porcelain, he eased down her high-cut pants to rest just below her hips, and exposed her blonde triangle of curls.

There was a sudden electric stillness in him. The potency of those earlier moments, the raw, pulsing passion, reignited. He cast her a knowing glance, almost as though he guessed her hunger to feel his lips there again, his clever seeking tongue.

'Patience,' he commanded, sitting back on his heels, a wicked laugh in his hot eyes, though there was a flush across his cheekbones.

Then, in deliberate provocation, he traced one mocking finger from her knee up the inside of her thigh, to where the skin was softer than silk. Rivulets of sensation thrilled beneath her sensitised skin, tormenting her inflamed flesh. She trembled in yearning for his smooth fingers to travel further, to extend that tingling delight and ease the insatiable, all-consuming hunger, but with a swift movement he whipped her pants all the way down to her ankles, then stood up.

The flagrantly sexual heat of his darkened gaze seared her to her core. She'd never felt so blazingly naked, or so wired to be appreciated.

'So, Goldilocks,' he said, appraising her flush, her stiffened nipples, with a challenging quirk of one brow. 'Do you want to run away from me now?' Despite his mockery there was a tear in his breathing that thrilled her to her feminine marrow.

She could play that game. She stepped out of her flimsy undies and kicked her dress aside. 'Only if you promise to chase me.' Her voice was smoky with desire. '*If* you think you can catch me.'

'I can catch you,' he growled at once, stepping forward and easily trapping her in his embrace.

But she slipped from his grasp and danced away from him, and, with her arms outstretched, pirouetted in her high heels, her hair flying out around her, taunting him, revelling in her nudity like a brazen siren. As he watched her, laughing, the flame that flared in his eyes revved her excitement to a wild pitch. She couldn't remember ever feeling so turned on, so joyous and wanton and abandoned. She wanted him to do everything to her, to ravish her to the limit and take her to paradise with his hard, athletic body.

She brought her fandango to a standstill, posing with her back to him. 'What do you think?' she taunted huskily, throwing him a glance over her shoulder.

Tom felt his laughter seize along with his lungs. Driven by the need to obliterate the intensifying black pain that threatened to engulf him, he fixed his every conscious nerve on her pale beauty.

The hot blood pounded a path to his groin as he took in the heavy hair brushing her white, shapely back, the alluring ridge of her spine. Slowly, he drank in the heart-stirring curves of neck and shoulder, the delicacy of her supple waist. His underclothes constricted him. He feasted his eyes on the gorgeous curves of her bottom, as smooth and exquisitely shaped as a peach.

Impossibly he hardened further, throbbing to penetrate that slim blonde beauty and bury himself in her sweet, vibrant flesh.

Gently he took her shoulders and turned her to face him.

'Luscious,' he said, his voice gravelled with lust.

Cate gasped in a breath. He wasn't playing now. His eyes were aflame. He pulled her against him and she felt the hard ridge of his erection against her belly. He slipped his hand under her chin to lift her face, and his mouth came down on hers in a searing kiss, as possessive and uncompromising as a conqueror's. As he pushed her towards the bed his marauding tongue thrust in to stroke hers in a graphic simulation of possession, driving her body to a raging awareness of an empty hollow desperate to be filled.

With her thirst still burning to be slaked, the sexy kiss broke as abruptly as it had started, the backs of her knees connecting with the bed, and she plumped down on its edge.

She surveyed him with wanton eyes while he unbuttoned his shirt and tossed it. Her mouth dried at the hard beauty of his bronzed chest, his powerful arms, the scattering of curled black hair that narrowed over the flat plane of his abdomen to disappear so alluringly below his navel.

Her mouth watered to taste him. In the grip of fever she reached up to caress his lean ribs, and, moaning, felt the scorching heat of the bronzed satin skin riding his taut muscles.

She panted for him.

A quiver rippled through him as she sought his belt buckle, but he captured her hands and put them firmly from him, frustrating her immediate need to enjoy him to the full, refusing to allow her any control.

It was maddening. It was torture. It was cruel deprivation.

But with a flash of that divine creativity he seemed to inspire in her, she rolled herself into the middle of the bed, and stretched out like a sensuous cat, casting him a long, tantalising glance as she ran her tongue-tip over her upper lip.

It worked. To her immense pleasure something like a flash-fire bolted through his body. His hot eyes riveted to her languid pose, he dragged off his shoes and socks, unbuckled his belt and stripped off his trousers and underpants.

For the first time she viewed him in the naked flesh. Her heart slowed to a heavy pounding beat, awed by his proud erect penis, its thick, virile length impressive. With appreciation she took in the sinewy grace of his long limbs, so muscular and satisfyingly hairy. The raw, masculine beauty of Tom Russell's lean frame grabbed at her heart and stirred the hot, throbbing ache between her legs, melting the coil of tension in her womb into a molten pool of yearning.

If he could be hers...

The lamp's glow warmed the smooth, supple undulations of her body to a pale golden shimmer, and Tom felt all the knifepoints of anguish that had gathered in him since he'd read his father's letter soothe. With a mental effort he thrust aside awareness of his wounds to concentrate on her beauty. Sweet forgetfulness beckoned like a mirage.

He stretched out beside her, urgent to drown himself in smiling blue-green eyes shadowed by passion. She turned on her side to receive him, and his hungry gaze devoured slender limbs and curves as smooth and graceful as an alabaster figurine.

He inhaled the fresh, clean scent of her skin. His rock-hard shaft throbbed for the sheath of her honeyed flesh, but he disciplined himself to wait, take her higher, and her release would be all the sweeter.

Despite his heavy heart, his pulse pumped a strong erotic beat as he pushed her onto her stomach. He traced the curve of her spine, relishing her skin's tingling fire under his fingers, the pleasure of pleasing her somehow an assuagement to his pain.

He grazed the hollow at the base of her spine with his lips, then, with sure, knowing hands, caressed the smooth contours of her buttocks. It was a challenge to stop, they were so achingly, meltingly desirable, and he struggled with his bitter-sweet need to take her there and then as he registered the little flinch that signalled her leap of response.

Lust and a need for immediate release threatened to overwhelm him as he gazed down at her. Her glorious hair was fanned out around her on the pillow like a glossy halo, but with her lips so tantalisingly parted, the allure of her languorous green eyes wrenched him as no angel ever could.

Resisting the temptation to rush her, he thanked the fates he'd been blessed with iron control.

'I believe I owe you,' he murmured, watching her eyes swirl with awareness, tracing her edible mouth with his thumb. He was scorchingly minded of those other lips, the dark crimson portals plump and glistening for him. 'I always pay my debts.'

She traced his collar-bone with a subtle hand, and beneath her sleepy lashes her eyes gleamed assent. She stretched out her slim arms, offering herself in such total surrender he thrilled to the promise of oblivion in her white body.

He started with little kisses, first her mouth, the delicate line of her jaw, then her throat and the valley between her breasts. Heartbreakingly beautiful, her breasts were full and firm, the nipples as red and ripe as strawberries. He tasted them, giving each a sly little teasing nip with his teeth. The electrified response that rippled through her slim form energised his own wild blood.

The words broke from him. 'I've never met a woman who affected me like you.'

Her wry, incredulous smile twisted something in his chest. Didn't she believe him? At once he needed to convince her. In some mysterious, primeval way, his inner sadness fused with an urgent need to embrace all that was bright and true and life-affirming. In the grip of some frenzied force, he was seized with a passion to make love to Cate Summerfield in earnest.

A warning voice piped up to remind him of the dangers of

getting involved but he blocked it out. With a fierce intensity he explored every curve and hollow of her smooth, pliant body, her every small writhe and sigh like anaesthesia to the aching hole in his chest. He used all the skills at his command to heighten her desire, deliberately inciting a trail of fire all the way across the gentle mound of her stomach and down to her silky tangle of curls.

He paused there, tantalising her anticipation. She stilled, and stayed motionless, her breath on hold, prickling with suspense, her longing almost tangible. He could feel her struggle with her pride, not to give in. Not to beg.

She said at last, her voice beguilingly hoarse, 'What now?'

He raised his head. With a charge of satisfaction he saw his own fire reflected in her shadow-darkened eyes.

'Now, I'm going to kiss you properly.'

To his complete amazement a long, slow blush suffused her upper chest and throat and washed into her cheeks. Intrigued, he stared at her for seconds, grappling with the vague implications. Who'd ever have expected Cate Summerfield to be shy? With tender amusement he kissed the patch of soft curls at the apex of her thighs and said silkily, 'Would you care to open for me?'

Her smouldering glance thrilled through him in a delicious communication of yearning mixed with uncertainty. It was so provocative. Tentatively she parted her thighs, a little at first, then wider, opening to him at last in such irresistible seduction, such utter, giving submission, he was moved with a passionate fervour to delight this warm, generous temptress and pleasure her to the hilt.

He positioned himself between her knees. Her erotic primal scent summoned his every masculine instinct with a compelling call. Red-hot, healthy blood surged to his groin.

First, he kissed her with his lips, enjoying the quivers of pleasure rippling through her. Then he raised the temperature with a tongue kiss, and ravished her with tender relish until her moist inner walls spun into a spasm that rocked through her body. He waited until her sobbing little sigh abated and she grew still, then slid up beside her.

Like the male animal he was, he burned to plunge his aching rod into her straight away and possess her slim white body until she bucked beneath him like a wild filly. Anything for blissful oblivion. But his conscience reminded him it was too soon for her. Give her time. Let her cool down a notch.

She lay silently for some moments, studying him almost as if she could read his mind—thank God no one ever would—then she roused him from his contemplation by placing her hand over his heart and whispering with earnest sincerity, 'That was truly the most intimate thing I've ever experienced.'

Jolted, he leaned up and gazed at her in bemused wonderment. What lacklustre lovers had she had in the past? Curiously touched, and at the same time reluctant to think about her with any other man, especially that cocky little ginger-haired guy, he kissed her lips, then dropped down again with his head beside hers on the pillow.

What was it about bringing a woman to orgasm that could move a man so deeply, shake him to the foundations, and make him feel so tender and protective? Although, he had to admit it hadn't happened to him before quite like this. Was it just him this dark night, or Cate Summerfield?

He was reminded then that she *needed* protection. Muttering an exclamation, he reached over to the drawer in his bedside table, searching till he found the packet that had lived there, unmolested, for two years.

He paused, the packet in his hand. Memories, sharp and unbidden, rose to the surface.

With her body taut and thrumming like a violin, pleasured, but, oh, so ready for more, Cate lay on her side, waiting. She saw him still, saw his lean, strong face clench and grow harsh. On an instinct she sat up, firmly took the packet from him and opened the wrapper.

Compelled by her grave, steady gaze, Tom choked back the past and allowed her to help him slide the condom onto his sweetly agonised shaft, her slim, pale fingers trembling.

His eyes lighted on her fingernails, unpainted and neatly trimmed. Her naturalness and lack of artifice moved him in a strangely poignant way. From somewhere the thought crept in—and he must have uttered it aloud, for it left a bloody gash as if it had been ripped from him—'He would have liked you. He wasn't always such a bad old guy.'

Her eyes widened, then filled with tears. 'Oh, Tom, Tom.' She put her hands on his shoulders, then moved onto his lap and kissed him deeply with her arms around him, her breasts pressed against his chest, cramming his aroused penis against her lower abdomen with maddening, torturous delight.

The scent and silky softness of her skin and hair tormented his senses unbearably. He blamed the alcohol, for her sweet compassion played unmercifully on the bizarre state he was in, and he felt as if there was so much more in her kiss than mere desire. At least, he needed there to be.

The tough, hardened shell locking in his pain threatened to crack and splinter open. As the kiss broke and he gazed at her he'd never have believed it possible that he, a man, could be composed of so much rawness. He tried to rationalise it, explain it to himself, but his brain felt like a boiling pot of things he was tired of thinking about.

The only thing he could be rock-sure of was that he felt deeply and overwhelmingly affected by Cate Summerfield. He heard himself saying, and he'd never meant it more, 'I want to make love to you. You're...of all the women I've known, you must be the sweetest... You're the one... The one I've been...I'll adore you for ever, Cate Summerfield. Do you know that?'

He seized her and pushed her down on the pillow. Her mouth was bruised from kissing, but he needed to kiss her again. There was no way he could stop. She responded at once with the same burning hunger he felt himself. He invaded the sweet interior of her mouth with his tongue, mingling their hot breaths in triumphant possession.

He broke from her and searched her eyes. They were dark, lustrous with anticipation. 'You're my lover now,' he rasped. 'I won't share you,'

Her eyes widened in surprise, and for an instant her shallow, panting little breaths suspended. Then he slid over her, he parted her thighs and took fierce possession of her soft yielding form.

He watched her face, thrilling when she closed her eyes as he entered her, her lashes perfect arcs against her cheeks. He heard himself groan with the intense, searing pleasure as her deliciously tight sheath closed around him.

Though yearning to lose himself in her vibrant body, he forced himself to move softly at first, to rock her gently into his rhythm. He controlled his straining urgency to let go. And although every stroke was the sweetest, sizzling torment, urging him on to harder, faster thrusts, he waited with her until he felt her taut body relax.

Then he felt the tension in her muscles give way to sensuality, felt her long, slim legs wrap around him to take him in further, heard her wrenching little cry of pleasure, and there was no more holding back.

Moving inside her sweet, honeyed flesh, he abandoned his bitter self, forgetful of grief and deceit. Possessing Cate Summerfield utterly suddenly seemed the purest of goals. It was an exhilarating ride to freedom. As he reached the glorious summit he felt her muscles contract into spasm around him, and knew the fabulous rapture of total release as his hot, life-giving seed spurted forth.

CHAPTER ELEVEN

THE SUNSHINE filtering through the silk drapes suggested that the day had advanced beyond early morning. Unfamiliar sounds drifted in, and Cate took a few seconds to realise where she was. Her eyes focused on the Streeton. Of course. Tom's bed, and she was alone in the tumbled sheets.

A clock on the cabinet showed it was close to ten. The evening before rushed back. Oh, God. What had she *done*?

Bathed in a heavy feeling of something world-shaking having happened, she sat up gingerly and put her hand to her head. So far, so good.

Gently, gently. The soles of her feet met the sensuous, silken Tree of Life and rested there with reassuring steadiness.

Satisfied her head could take it, she padded into the bathroom and stood for long, satisfying minutes under soothing hot water. There was a pleasing soreness between her legs, and her insides melted in recollection. Her heart beat faster as images began to sharpen in her mind. Tom in bed, his strong arms around her. How sexy and tender he'd been, though there'd been such pain behind his smile.

She was overwhelmed with the sense of something powerful and intense having taken place between them, far beyond mere sex. Some of the things he'd said had been so beautiful, so full of promise, she hardly dared to dwell on them for fear of jinxing the possibilities. She hoped they weren't just uttered in the heat of the moment, to be repudi-ated in the cold light of day.

She wrapped herself in a white towelling bathrobe left hanging behind the door, and hugged it to herself in case Tom had worn it before her.

She pulled off the shower cap and studied her face in the mirror for signs of wear and tear. Apart from puffy pink lips, her skin looked surprisingly fresh, her eyes clear and bright. Despite the late night, and her tremulous hopes, she felt as chirrupy as a starling. And ravenous.

At the door she hesitated, conscious of a certain apprehen-sion, then walked out, the bathrobe trailing, her bare feet soundless on the boards. A glass jug of orange juice had been placed on the kitchen bench, and there was a promising fra-grance of coffee. She helped herself to the juice, and took it with her in search of Tom.

She found him in the dining room with the blinds drawn, amid a sea of newspapers. He was brooding into space, his black brows heavily lowered, painkillers and coffee at his elbow, a broadsheet spread before him on the table. She saw at once it was the *Clarion*. He was barefoot, in jeans and a black vest, his bare bronzed arms and a day's growth of dark beard giving him a bad-boy sexiness that clutched unbearably at her insides.

Tom raised his eyes. Wrapped in his bathrobe, Cate Summerfield looked as fresh and radiant as the spring morning. Though his throat felt as parched as the Simpson Desert, his testosterone levels perked up and he forced a growl. 'Hello… How—how are you?'

A cloud of some soapish, feminine fragrance wafted his way.

'Fine, thank you. Never better. Excellent, in fact. Did you—did you sleep well?'

He hesitated. He had a stirring flash of that instant before sleep had overwhelmed him, her lissom body pressed against him so she could hold him. So he could feel her heartbeat.

'Certainly.' Perhaps he sounded gruff, even a little defensive, but a man had his dignity.

She bent and lightly kissed him on the forehead, and more of the heady scent rose from the valley between her breasts. His blood stirred to the knowledge that she was probably naked under that robe.

Cate pulled out a chair, noticing him flinch at the minuscule scrape on the floorboards. 'Sorry.' There was heaviness in the lines around his eyes. 'Do you have a headache?'

He waved his denial but she wasn't convinced. The painkillers suggested otherwise. And his coffee looked virtually untouched. He lowered his gaze to the *Clarion*. Shutting her out. She scanned the columns upside down. He'd gone beyond the front page, so she had no clue as to whether her story had made it. Was that why he looked so forbidding? She scrolled through what she'd written in her head. What had she said that he wouldn't like?

She sat down, and her body surged with remembrance of the night's passions. His bare bronzed, muscular arms were so tempting she had to fold hers on the table to stop herself from reaching across to maul him. She examined him covertly in search of a clue to the correct morning-after tone. She had the distinct feeling he wasn't concentrating on his reading.

'Er…Cate—' he drew a long breath '—look…I should apologise.' With a grimace he raised his eyes to hers. 'Last night. I had a bit to drink. I don't usually…but I'm not making excuses. There is no excuse. Don't—er—read too much into anything I might have said.' A flush darkened his bristly cheek.

Her heart took a dive. 'Oh. You mean—about me being your lover?' As for him adoring her for ever… This didn't seem like the time to bring it up.

He gave her a quick startled glance, then returned his saturnine gaze to the paper, his mouth sternly compressed. She sensed turbulence in the airwaves. Surely he couldn't really be reading.

She grappled with her disappointment. He wouldn't be the first man to regret the romantic things he'd said. What could she expect? They'd only just met, for God's sake. Just because there'd been moments that had moved *her* quite intensely… She supposed now he couldn't wait to get rid of her.

Or maybe he'd gone dramatically off her after reading the article. If it had been published. Suddenly her burning need to know asserted itself.

'Is that the *Clarion,* Tom?'

He glanced up at her, then closed the paper and handed it across.

With trembling hands she whipped it around to the front page. Halfway down blazed Mike's best shot, the grim one of Tom arriving in the car park. Under the headline 'HEIR STEPS INTO BIG SHOES'—the copy editor's words—was her name, followed by the first section of her story. The rest was continued on page seven, alongside a photo spread. She stared, marvelling for fabulous seconds as her precious words leaped out at her.

People all over New South Wales would read it. *Gran* would read it. And in tiny, elegant print at the top of the three magnificent little columns they would read *Cate Summerfield.*

She felt the quick rush of tears and her heart gave such a bound she had to hold herself stiff for fear of it bursting through her chest wall. But, searingly conscious of the grim subject of her piece sitting right there, she sat holding the paper with both hands and maintained her poker face, until something gave her the courage to glance at him. His mouth had relaxed its sternness, and he was watching her, his eyes glinting with such knowing amusement, she felt encouraged.

'Er…I hope you didn't find what I said too—confronting.'

'Not at all,' he growled politely. 'I so enjoy your pithy style.'

She couldn't prevent a grin from breaking through her mist, but it wasn't nearly enough, and the fabulous joy bubbled up inside her until she was forced to spring up out of her chair and wave the paper in the air while she danced a few ecstatic steps.

'Oh,' she cried. 'This is good. It's so good, Tom. It's really, really *good*.'

Tom Russell laughed, then winced and put his hands to his temples. Then, exactly as if he wasn't suffering the most vicious headache in Sydney, he got up out of his chair and grabbed her around the waist and kissed her, scraping her face with his bristly jaw in the most satisfying and sexy way. *Not* the kiss of a man eaten up with regrets.

'Explain to me,' he growled, holding her, 'what a man's socks have to do with anything. Only a rag like the *Clarion* would publish such half-baked psychobabble.'

'The most widely read rag in the country,' she crowed. 'The thinking man's rag. The rag that carries the culture of a nation.'

'The rag that'd collapse at the first sign of some half-decent competition,' he retorted caustically.

'Ah,' she taunted, giddy and aroused from the kiss, 'but where will that come from?'

He stared frowningly down at her for a second, then released her. Rubbing his jaw, he excused himself, murmuring something about shaving. She uncurled her toes. Even hungover and unshaven, she could have eaten him alive.

'Try some of that orange juice,' she risked calling after him.

She'd only brought the one change of clothes, a shortish skirt and a white top to wear under a light sky-blue cardy. After she'd dressed and applied a discreet measure of make-up, she retrieved her things from the evening before and packed them into her overnight bag.

Tom strolled out, showered, clean-shaven and fresh-smelling. She noted that the jug of orange juice stood empty.

His sharp eye fell on her bag at once. 'Where are you going with that?'

She hesitated. 'Home. One night was what we agreed.'

'It was…' He rubbed his ear. 'Only I'm not sure that would be for the best. What about tonight.'

'Tonight?'

'Well, we haven't accomplished everything we need to do.'

'Oh.' A wild little hope raised its head. 'You mean—convincing Malcolm Devlin?'

'Who? No, no. To hell with Malcolm Devlin. I wondered if you might like to come to a concert with me. Apparently there's a guy playing who's amazing on his Strativarius. And then, tomorrow, I thought we might drive up to the farm. We'll need an early start, so you—you might want to stay over. If you'd like.' A gleam lit his eyes.

'Oh.' *Would* she. Thrilling through to her ecstatic core, she still managed to sound demure. 'Well, thank you. That would be—very nice. But I've only brought enough clothes for now. I'll have to go home and get a few more. And I…I will have to go and see my grandmother later. She'll be so excited about my front pager.'

'Right. I'll drive you.' He surveyed her from the ankles up with an intense gaze. 'You won't need different clothes for now, though, will you? What you're wearing is fine for today.' His deep voice deepened even further. 'You look—fine.'

It was so intensely flattering she couldn't help flushing with pleasure as his hot scrutiny roused every skin cell in her body. 'Fine,' she said in a breathless attempt to sound breezy. 'And what are we doing today?'

'I have some urgent matters to attend to. And I have to check over some properties.'

A delicious breakfast was served in Tom's private dining room downstairs. It must have fixed his headache because afterwards he looked refreshed and handsome, his grey eyes sparkling with purpose. And he must have been feeling energetic, because afterwards up in the suite when she'd cleaned her teeth, he strolled into the bathroom just as she was reapplying her dark red lipstick, and seemed galvanised by the sight.

He grabbed her and pushed her up against the vanity and kissed her mouth with greedy, lustful passion. At once the smouldering flame inside her roared into blazing life. To her intense excitement he started swiftly to undress her.

Instantly she was moist with desire. As his hands pushed up her sweater and sought the catch on her bra she breathed into his neck, 'What about your urgent matters?'

His voice thickened. 'Nothing is as urgent as this.'

She helped as well as she could. Her trembling hands flew clumsily to unbuckle his belt and struggle with the buttons on his shirt. Her eye was caught by disturbing flashes of their reflections in the mirrors as they each got in the other's way in their fever for skin contact.

Thrilling to the touch of his lean, bronzed hands on her bare breasts and bottom, she kicked away her fallen skirt and panties. She clung to him, avid for the faint salty taste of his skin on her tongue, and licked his flat nipples. His shuddering moan shivered through her like an aphrodisiac, and her excitement mounted as his hot hands slid between her legs.

She caught a glimpse of her face in the glass. A different woman was reflected there. A wild creature with blazing eyes.

'Wait, wait,' she gasped as he lifted her onto the marble vanity. She needn't have worried. He produced a foil packet from a lower drawer, then dragged off his clothes and laid his magnificent self bare.

He was so big and hard. She closed her hand around his hot, steel-and-velvet shaft and felt the deep quiver of response roil through him. She saw his eyes on the patch of blonde hair at the juncture of her thighs, and with a burning hunger to feel his hard length inside her, parted them in enticement.

He slipped on the protection, then lifted her legs to encircle his hips and thrust into her. Oh, the fabulous, searing pleasure. His thick, virile length filled her so satisfyingly she had to cry out. Then in full erotic view in the mirror he rocked her, his hot, urgent rhythm sending shafts of rapture like sunlight to pierce every nerve in her aroused body. They were spurred on by the sensual reflections of their coupling, and their urgency became so brisk and frantic, she needed to adjust her position on the bench.

But, barely missing a stroke, he pulled her closer, supporting her with his powerful arms around her back, while she locked her arms around his strong neck. She felt so exhilaratingly filled and embraced, with his chest in erotic friction with her breasts, that the sizzling rhythm rocketed her pleasure to the heights to explode in pure, white-hot ecstasy.

That was in the bathroom.

In the bedroom, *she* made love to *him* on the Tree of Life. Then, although she cherished the feel of him on her skin, when he suggested a bath she was more than willing. And in the spa he showed her wicked ways she'd never have dreamed possible.

'Is Malcolm Devlin really coming here?' she said afterwards, leaning back against his warm chest in the bubbles, feeling his lips on her neck as his powerful arms held her in a dreamy, blissful embrace.

'Probably not,' he allowed, tickling her ear with his hot breath.

She smiled to herself. 'What about your merger?'

His hands cupped her breasts. 'One thing at a time. Now I want to concentrate on my lover. I might have to keep you here for a while.'

Those words were so casual on his dark velvet tongue, but they thrilled her to the core.

In the afternoon he drove her to his father's house, an imposing four-storey mansion in Double Bay. A housekeeper warmly greeted Tom, then retired to her own apartments and left them alone.

Inside the big ground-floor living room Cate took it all in— the chandeliers, vast spaces and sumptuous furnishings. She gazed wide-eyed at a giant mediaeval tapestry that covered the wall from one floor to the next in the stairwell of the grand staircase.

If Gran could see her here. She pushed the notion away with a faint feeling of guilt.

She noticed Tom's sudden silence, and hung back when he approached the stairs. 'I'll wait down here,' she offered, not wanting to intrude.

He paused, his hand on the banister, then nodded. 'If you'd prefer.'

He was gone for some time. She wondered what sort of communion he was having with his father's things. She drifted into a pleasant room where French windows opened onto a green velvet lawn. For an instant beneath the scents of furniture polish and leather upholstery, she thought she could detect the faintest whiff of tobacco in the air, like the smoke from a passing cigar.

When Tom returned he looked calm and composed. 'Would you like to see it all before it's sold?'

She widened her eyes. 'You're selling it?'

He nodded. 'I have to decide what to keep, if anything. I guess I'll have to find a day to sort through his things.'

'Oh.' She felt inadequate to express her concern. 'This must be very painful for you.'

He ruffled his hair, frowning, then shrugged. 'It is, though strangely enough it's not as bad as I expected. They're only things, after all.'

Strolling through opulent rooms furnished in a bizarre mix of styles and periods to reflect the various tastes of its former mistresses, she felt secretly appalled. The sheer, extravagant waste of wealth.

They paused in the middle of the ballroom on a scale grand enough to grace some European palace. 'Did you really hold balls here?'

'Different events, when my mother was alive. After she died my father lost interest in entertaining. This was a great place for indoor cricket.' He turned an amused glance on her. 'You don't approve?'

She gave her head a wry shake. 'My grandmother sold her cottage to buy me a decent education. How could I?'

Next he drove her to a house by the sea. This one was modern, on a much simpler scale. On three levels, it was cunningly built into the northern side of a headland to protect it from the big southerlies. It overlooked the charming seaside suburb of Tamarama, its wide decks and windows open to spectacular views of the ever-changing sea. The house looked deserted, its gardens overgrown.

In the car Tom glanced at her, and, sensing his hesitation, she said quickly, 'Would you rather I wait here?'

'No, no.' He stirred himself and briskly got out of the car, then came round to open her door. He stopped on the paved path to survey the gardens with a frown, then ushered her onto the portico and through the front door.

The house was empty of furnishings. It had a pleasing entrance hall and cool, spacious rooms with tiled floors and high ceilings. She noticed the faint scent of sawdust, as if there hadn't been time to overlay the construction smells with the accumulated resonances of day-to-day living.

'This must be cool in summer,' she observed, her voice echoing in the empty space. 'Did your father like it here?'

'This wasn't his house. I built this one.'

'Oh.' She followed him from room to room, then returned to the first floor and strolled out onto the pool terrace. She leaned against the railing, and her eye drifted down over the descending rooftops and intervening shrubberies to the breakers smashing themselves against the rocks. The breeze whipped her hair around, and she used her sunglasses to hold it back from her face. 'Wow. How could you not live here? With these views, and all the lovely spaces, and that kitchen and the verandas.' She spread her hands. 'Don't you like it?'

He joined her and stood frowning down at the scene below, his hands shoved in his pockets. After a while he broke the silence. 'I designed this after I came back from England. My wife was involved in a research project there. I wanted her to come back to a real home, so…' He shrugged. 'She never came back. She never even saw this house.'

'Oh. I'm so sorry,' she said weakly. Her heart started to pound, as if she'd accidentally stumbled into a pit loaded with sharp, jagged spikes and they were all pressing into her chest. She swallowed to push one down that had lodged in her throat. 'That's such a tragedy, Tom,' she said croakily. 'I'm sure— I'm sure she would have loved it.'

He hunched his shoulders against the breeze. 'No, she wouldn't have.'

Cate stared down at the shore. People dotted the beach. A couple strolled along with a toddler between them, each holding one small hand. Suddenly Tom Russell's grief had a tangible reality. Was this what he'd wanted, what he'd lost?

She felt a terrible choking fear as something she'd been holding at bay at the edge of her mind sprang forward. Her eyes teared up and she slipped down her glasses to cover them, and turned away from the view. Away from the happy families playing on the beach. She forced herself to speak lightly, not let on her sudden cold dread.

'Why do you say that? That she wouldn't have? Because of her project?'

Sensing something in her voice, Tom glanced at her. Beneath the sunglasses her ripe, sensuous mouth was tense. He toyed with the possibility of telling the truth for once. His brain framed the forbidden words and unexpectedly he felt them rise to his tongue in an overpowering urge to escape.

'Not just the project,' he heard himself say without undue emotion. 'She met someone else over there and didn't want to leave him.'

The unbearable truth that had cut him to bloody ribbons hung for a second in the bright air, then dissipated. He made a swift mental examination of his interior for pain, but it felt amazingly neutral. He felt like a man who had been through a firestorm and survived. At last his anger and sadness over Sandra seemed finally to have worn out, like an old song played too often.

He slipped his arm around Cate Summerfield's slim waist and pulled her against him. His thoughts flew to the evening ahead with a pleasant surge of anticipation.

The trip back was subdued. Cate noticed Tom glance at her a couple of times, as if trying to read her expression, and smiled brightly at him.

After the splendours of some of his prime Sydney real estate, she'd tried to dissuade him from driving her back to the Lady Musgrave for her clothes. It wasn't just her craven reluctance for him to witness her ordinary circumstances. As she drew nearer to her own world her own pressing realities surfaced. How would she get rid of him so she could slip away to Gran?

She tried to insist that it would be more time-efficient if she were to catch the ferry over the water and back, but he wouldn't hear of her taking such a risk. She could have laughed in his face if it hadn't been so touching. It only seemed to illustrate the massive differences between them.

She sat tensely in her seat as he drove her across the bridge, aware her time was running out. Yesterday it had been such wild, exciting fun, acting as his girlfriend. Now she could see emotional devastation looming. She should have known. She knew what Marge would have said. A man in love with his dead wife might seek solace from a bit of live flesh, but it would only be a fling. She clenched her hands in her lap. That was what she was into, what she'd *known* all along she was plunging into. A sweet, poignant, passionate fling. With a man from a totally different background, who probably thought of her as a chick from the wrong side of the tracks.

The car drew to a halt and it homed in upon her that they had arrived in the driveway of the Lady Musgrave, without her having given any directions. She saw Tom examining the house. Despite her personal Summerfield brand of chutzpah, embarrassment crept into her cheeks. She toyed with the idea of pretending it wasn't a boarding house, just a rather faded mansion she happened to rent, then dismissed it. Even he might know the difference.

Why did those second floor balconies have to sag? Snatches of the bright, careless chat she'd heard at the memorial lunch echoed in her mind. Everyone in Sydney knew that in Tom Russell's circle property was everything. She angled her face away from him, reluctant to see contempt in his eyes.

But he was craning his neck for a better look. 'Aren't they lovely, these old places? Look at the detail on those gables. Aren't you lucky to have found it?'

She was gobsmacked. Totally rocked off her foundations. She stared at him, then wonderingly up at the house, looking through the peeling white paintwork for the first time at the house's gracious lines. It *was* beautiful. How could she not have noticed? It was a work of art.

She felt such a passionate rush of warmth for Tom Russell, she had to hold herself still a second or two before she could speak steadily enough not to give herself away. 'How—how did you know where I lived?'

'My security people looked you up yesterday. I drove by here last night, thinking I might save you a trip on the ferry.'

'*Did* you? What time was that?'

'Just after eight.'

She wrinkled her brow. 'I'd have been here then.'

'You were. You were talking to someone. I didn't stop because you seemed so—involved.'

Steve. Her eyebrows flew up. 'Oh.'

His acute gaze raked her face. She knew how it could have looked and was annoyed to feel herself flush. 'That was nothing. Just a stupid misunderstanding.'

He was silent, his silence having a sharp listening edge that made her feel forced to explain further.

'Look, covering the memorial was a big deal for me. Steve

used it as a pretext to come over last night to talk.' She rolled her eyes, conscious of Tom's cool, steady scrutiny.

'To talk about—what?' he said casually. 'Resuming your engagement?'

'Not exactly. Just—just…' She shrugged. 'Well, all right. Something like that.'

'And do you want to?'

'Oh, please.' Beneath his black lashes his grey gaze was unreadable. She searched his lean, stern face, the faint crease between his brows. How could he ask such a question? After last night, how could he even *think*—?

He said mildly, 'If the engagement is over, why can't he get over it and move on? What does he hope to get from you, visiting you at home?'

She stared at him in surprise. 'What do you mean—*if* the engagement's over? Steve just feels guilty about something that happened, that's all. That's what he can't get over.'

'Ah. The mistake he made.'

She held down her irritation with a calming breath and said lightly, 'What is this, the Spanish Inquisition? I hope you aren't imagining I might still be seeing him.'

He stared out at the street for a second, then brought his grave gaze back to hers. 'After last night, how could I think that?'

He leaned over and brushed her lips with his, the light touch of his fingers on her jaw sending shivers of yearning through her willing flesh.

Her heart surged with pleasure to know that last night meant so much to him. It was close to an acknowledgement that something real was happening between them.

But she had to admit to a slight feeling of shock. What had he suspected—that she was capable of carrying on with Steve and him at the same time? It showed a lack of confidence in her. And if she *had* been cheating… A chill touched her spine like the first breath of winter. There'd been uncompromising steel in that uncomfortable little grilling.

His arms slid around her and the kiss turned deep and sexual. When at last he let her go, she felt breathless, her breasts warm and aroused. Stirred into wanting him again, she was reluctant to tear herself away, and had to force herself to open her door.

'Anyway,' she said, her low, firm tone for herself as much as for him, 'I don't want you to wait now. After I collect my things I want to visit my grandmother. I'll be back in time for the concert, I promise. Honestly.'

He leaned towards her. 'But—'

'No, no, I'm serious.' She got out before he could argue, then walked around to his side. She bent to his open window and swiftly kissed his lips, slipping her tongue through to his, and breathing, 'Can't wait for tonight, lover.'

Stirred by that last brief, delicious tangle of tongues, Tom watched her run up the drive and disappear into the house. But as he drove back across the bridge, a thought struck him. Hadn't she just visited her grandmother?

CHAPTER TWELVE

GRAN WAS as thrilled by Cate's front pager as she was herself. While they marvelled over it, Cate couldn't stop beaming and breaking off to hug her and thank her for all the times she'd encouraged her to stay strong when journalism had seemed too hard. She wished she could tell her about Tom. There was so much about him she knew her grandmother would like. But the risk was too great. How would Gran take it, that she'd fallen in love with Tom Russell?

The visit must have been a bit too exciting, because although Gran joked about her frailty, there was a bluish tinge around her mouth and she had to take a few puffs of her oxygen. And after they'd said goodbye, before Cate left she glanced back into the ward and saw with a fearful pang that her grandmother looked dreadfully tired and pale. The heart-stopping thought struck her that Gran was sinking.

She could die before her operation.

She managed to make it back to Tom's in time for the concert. She sat beside him in the fifth row of the Recital Hall in Angel Place, thrilling to the music and the gorgeous man, enjoying the occasional brush of his sleeve on her arm. Afterwards he took her to a small Italian restaurant in Paddington, but they didn't linger long. They wolfed their food and drove home, replete with their fill of music and drunk on the desire flowing between them. And, as though possessed with an insatiable hunger, Tom made passionate love to her until their lips were bruised and their bodies aching for sleep.

They didn't go to the farm on Sunday. There wasn't time. And she didn't go back to her place. She stayed and made love with Tom. And when Monday rolled around, she walked down to the Quay and caught the bus to work, just as if she weren't living with a billionaire.

Every day after that became a mad tightrope act between work, Gran and rushing home to Tom, sometimes twice in the day. Tom would call her at work, or wherever Harry had sent her, to meet him for a stolen, frantic hour of passion and she was always so excited, so energised by her romantic double life, she couldn't resist.

'I'm downstairs,' he'd murmur from the car, 'Quick. I want to touch you.'

She knew she was risking discovery by her colleagues, but the risk made the pleasure all the more exhilarating. She'd slip from her building and run to the nearby sidestreet where he waited, double-parked, to speed her back to the hotel for love.

And it was love, on her side. Once she'd half acknowledged it to herself she'd plunged deeply into that thrilling, treacherous sea. On Tom's side she couldn't be sure. She had a dim understanding that his passion for her was bound up with the extraordinary circumstances of that first night. A small, fearful part of her suspected it could evaporate as suddenly as it had appeared. Her heart was suspended in a joyous, tingling trance, and she had a battle to keep her battered old hopes and dreams locked in their cave.

'Maybe we should stretch out the time between bouts,' she said one lunch hour, lying naked in his powerful arms in the dreamy haze of afterglow. 'Maybe we'll burn ourselves out.'

'I'll never stop burning for you,' he said instantly, his voice thick and fierce. 'I'll never have enough of you.'

Was that a promise? She wished she dared to ask. At work, she couldn't wait for the evenings. She'd catch the train, fulfil her commitment to Gran, and rush back to Tom's before he arrived home. The giddy days flew by so fast, her secret was so fantastic, she was afraid to stop and question where it was heading. His passion for her was real. Let that be enough.

When Tom was away from her, he felt as though his all-consuming desire had somehow liberated something in his brain. He found himself questioning just how much of his empire he really wanted to keep. Some of his father's holdings he'd never personally liked, and he made some ruthless judgements about unloading them. He negotiated discreet sales of the yacht, several overseas properties and embarked on a deal to release the hotel chain. At the same time he put everything in train for the merger needed to grease the wheels of his media company. But always at the edge of his mind was the knowledge that Cate Summerfield was at home, her lusciousness his for the taking, waiting for him to bury himself in her silken warmth.

Well, usually she was.

Sometimes on week-nights she was delayed. She made no explanation, and it wasn't his right to question her, but he wondered.

Late one Saturday afternoon he arrived back from some negotiations to find her on her way out.

'Gran,' she explained after a small hesitation.

'I'll drive you. Isn't it time I meet the family?' He was only half serious, but though she made a laughing refusal he thought he glimpsed in her eyes a fleeting alarm. He supposed she *was* visiting her grandmother. Where else would she be going?

He listened sometimes for news of that guy. She spoke of her other colleagues after her day's work, but never mentioned him. He wondered why that was, because he knew she saw the guy. He'd seen them coming out of her building together one lunch time when he'd driven around there with the intention of snatching a stolen hour with her. They'd strolled along talking for a few minutes, then the guy had walked off in another direction.

Cate was thrilled when Tom casually suggested a trip up to his farm. She'd sensed how close the farm was to his heart. Surely it must mean something, that he was prepared to share this part of his life with her. They left very early on a Sunday morning, driving north along the Pacific Highway, then west to wend their way through the farms and vineyards of the Hunter Valley. Eventually Tom turned the car into a long avenue of tall poplars. Behind miles of wooden fencing, Cate saw horses grazing the green pastures.

Tom's farm was no small holding. It was an extensive horse stud, nestled in a lush valley between the Hunter River and the foothills of the purple mountains.

Pancakes and coffee awaited them on the veranda of the rambling homestead, then Tom drove her all over in a big SUV, and showed her the thoroughbred mares waiting for their mates to be flown in from around the world. Wherever they stopped the Jeep, horses trotted over to the fence, jostling to push their noses in through her open window for a pat, their dark liquid eyes warm and inquisitive. In the home paddock newborn foals tottered after their mothers on spindly legs. Cate was enchanted.

She could see how Tom kept his lean, bronzed fitness. He looked at home there. In his jeans and tee-shirt, discussing farm business with his manager, or sitting easily astride his own big stallion on a ride to visit the head vet, while Cate clung nervously to the sweet-natured mare provided for her, it was clear he was in frequent residence at the farm.

Lunch was a picnic with Tom's manager and his wife and children on the bank of a pebbly creek. Tom sent all the kids scouting for twigs and branches while he built a small campfire, and to Cate's awestruck amazement he boiled the billy for tea. There were sandwiches packed by the cook, fruit cake and sweet juicy mandarins, washed down with the strong black bushman's brew.

It was a pleasant, good-humoured event. After they'd eaten,

conversing drowsily in the early afternoon heat, the last curls of blue smoke drifting around them, Tom leaned back against a log and pulled Cate against him. She could have stayed there for ever beside the creek, listening to the stories about Tom's boyhood experiences at the farm, enjoying the lazy laughter, Tom's jaw grazing her forehead, her hand relaxed on his muscular thigh. She imagined with pleasant torment how it might have been if they'd been alone there in the shade. Would his hand have strayed beneath the waistband of her jeans? Would they have made love on the leaf-strewn grass?

He murmured to her, his voice husky, and she knew he was thinking the same thing. 'Did you know your hair smells of mandarin?'

When the shadows started to lengthen, they all strolled back to the house, Tom holding her hand. After the others had gone, he put his arms around her. 'What a torture that was. They're such great people, but all I ever want is to have you to myself.'

Her heart thrilled to the words. 'Ditto.'

She'd never felt more at one with him. This was love. Surely it was love.

She pressed herself against him, her arms tight around him. 'Oh, it's been such a gorgeous day. I never want it to end. But it has to, I'm afraid.' Her regret welled up in her voice. 'What a shame we have to go home.'

He relaxed his hold and smiled down at her. 'We don't have to yet. Wouldn't you like to stay tonight? It's always so pleasant here. And it's still chilly enough for a fire in the evenings.' He drew her close and murmured in her ear, his deep voice velvet and seductive. 'I haven't seen you by fire-light yet. We'll have some dinner, tell each other the stories of our lives—if we have *time*, of course—keep each other warm in that big old four-poster, and get up with the birds to drive back early in the morning. You haven't experienced this place unless you've seen it at birdsong.'

Pressed into his hard body, imprisoned by his long muscled limbs, his masculine scent arousing her senses with its faint infusion of woodsmoke, she was sorely tempted. Imagining the night in his arms in that heavenly-looking bed made her veins flow with yearning. 'I'd love to, honestly. But I can't. I have to…there's something I've promised to do.'

There was a sudden tension in the big frame holding her. But he spoke easily. 'Ah. Someone you have to meet?'

She hesitated. 'Well, yes. My grandmother.'

He held her away from him, scanning her face with a narrowed gaze. 'But—didn't you say you saw her yesterday? Wouldn't she understand if you phoned to let her know?'

There was an inflection in his voice, and she knew she must sound like a bore. For a moment she even considered his suggestion. She supposed she could phone Autumn Leaves. Beg one of the busy staff to find the time for Gran. Except…

'No. No, I promised.' His frown deepened, and she drew away from him, adding in a small, remorseful voice, 'Honestly. She isn't very well. I do need to see her.'

'I see.' He gave a light shrug. 'Well, then. In that case, we'd better be on our way.'

On the trip back, Tom tried to concentrate all his attention on the driving. But he was only human. He still had a brain, despite his insatiable, never-ending desire, and it would have been insane of him not to at least weigh up the evidence.

He asked her a few searching questions about her grandmother's health, and her answers were plausible. Very plausible. It all fitted. A warm, generous woman like Cate *would* visit her ailing grandmother every day. And she'd already proven herself to be as straight as a die. Why else would she have come back that first Friday evening? And when he thought of the fantastic, intense connection, the transforming passion…

It *had* to mean as much to her. She couldn't be faking it.

Although…women did.

He glanced at her. She turned her head and met his gaze with an anxiety that made his chest pang.

'You're disappointed. You're not angry with me, are you?'

'No, no. Not at all,' he said warmly. And he wasn't. Not angry, anyway. Disappointed…? Perhaps. He was loath to return to the harsh reality of the working week.

He had no right to doubt her, like some obsessed Othello. If she hadn't been a reporter… If he hadn't seen her that fateful night, talking to that little guy who went after stories like a fox terrier…the guy she'd been involved with.

A heaviness invaded his heart. In spite of himself, he had to ask the unaskable question. *Had been* involved with him, or still was?

He glanced at her profile. She was chewing her lower lip, her hands twisting in her lap. Worrying about her gran. Or…? His gut tightened. Was she in fact wondering how to get rid of him so she could safely meet her accomplice? Her—the word speared him—*lover*?

He pushed the thought away. It was pure paranoia. Just because once or twice…

Forget it. In a very short time she'd be proving him wrong and directing him to her grandmother's front door. If she didn't, if she evaded that, he'd have to really start wondering.

Almost without him noticing it, they reached the city. The machine purred through the outskirts with its legendary smoothness. As they cruised through the northern suburbs she said suddenly, 'If you could just drop me off at my place, Tom, I'll catch a taxi over to Gran's from there.'

His insides clenched like a fist. Here it was. As far as he knew she hadn't been home to her boarding house for weeks, so why would she need to go now?

Though his lungs were in a stranglehold, he kept his voice smooth enough. 'Your place? Wouldn't it be easier for me to drive you to your grandmother's?'

She hesitated, then gave him one of those clear, straight

glances. 'There's a few things I need to pick up. Then I might freshen up and change, and… Well, I—I need to see Gran on my own. You understand.'

'Yes,' he said drily. 'I think I do.' The words tasted like bile on his tongue.

He drew up at the Lady Musgrave, and turned his mocking gaze on her. Unaware of the vice gripping his chest, she leaned over and pressed her lips to his. Why did the kiss of betrayal always taste sweetest of all? Swiftly she opened her door and got out.

He gripped the wheel, anger and some other nameless emotion churning in his chest, then without another glance at her drove on up the street to the roundabout. He was forced to wait there several minutes, his fingers drumming the wheel as he pictured her running upstairs to wash off all traces of *him* before stepping into her lover's arms. When he eventually drove back he was in time to see her climb into a cab.

Contrary to what she'd told him, she'd made no attempt to change her clothes. Too urgent to get there. A grim feeling of inevitability gripped him. One way or the other, he had to know.

He slowed to allow enough distance, then followed the taxi.

In her anxiety to see Gran, Cate nearly ran through Reception, down the hall and into the ward. Gran was sitting up doing a cryptic crossword, her earphones on so she didn't have to listen to constant replays of mall music. When she saw Cate her face lit up, as always. Cate kissed her, then sat on the steel chair and examined her closely.

Gran had news. She'd been informed that her number had come up at last and her operation was slated for some time in the next month. Cate was listening to the details with mixed feelings when she noticed a tall shadow in the periphery of her gaze. She looked over at the ward entrance and her lungs nearly froze with shock. Tom was standing there, scanning the ward.

After a moment's stunned immobility, she sprang up from her chair and flew across the room, threading her way around the beds and the small scattering of faithful Sunday visitors. Tom smiled when he saw her, but before he could speak she grabbed his arm and pulled him into the hall.

'You can't come here,' she muttered urgently. 'You mustn't be here.'

His black brows shot up. Surprise registered in his eyes. 'I mustn't?'

'No. Please leave, Tom. Now. Right now.' She gave him a sharp little push, anything to get him out of Gran's view.

Involuntarily, Tom fell back a few paces. He spread his hands. 'I'm sorry. I didn't mean to…but there's something I want to…'

'Just leave, will you?' Cate glanced back to see if he was still in Gran's line of vision. 'I don't think she saw you, but that doesn't mean someone else won't. Just go now. I'll… we'll talk later.'

He'd moved beyond the entrance to the ward, and she tried pushing him further, but met the implacable resistance of a body larger and more solid than hers. She gathered her strength for a greater effort, but he grabbed her arms and held her still.

'Don't push.' His voice, though gentle, held steel. 'It's too late. She has seen me. I think now you'll just have to introduce me.'

Alarmed, she just blurted what came into her head. 'Absolutely not. Her health is fragile. I have to be very, very careful who I bring here.'

The stunned look in his eyes sent a rush of remorse to her heart, but in a matter of life and death she knew what she had to do.

She glanced about her as people came and went, aware she and Tom were attracting curious glances. Panic gripped her. 'Please,' she begged, gasping for breath as if she'd been in a race. 'It would worry her if she thought I was with—'

His eyes glinted. 'Me.'

He said it so quietly she flushed.

Realising at last that she was causing damage here, she caught his hand. 'Tom,' she said, her voice strained with distress, 'can we please go outside?'

Outside, they faced each other in the light from the windows. Tom's lean face was serious and unsmiling. In desperation to explain before disaster became irrevocable, she scrabbled for the words.

'I'm sorry, Tom, so—so sorry.' She placed a hand on his arm in supplication. 'You see, Gran's heart is unable to sustain a shock. That's why she has to stay here while she waits for her operation. And if she thought I was seeing *you*—' A thought struck her. 'How did you know I was here?'

He didn't reply and she stared at him, uncomprehending for several seconds. Then she understood. 'You followed me.'

A flush darkened his cheeks, but he met her gaze steadily. 'I wanted to see where your grandmother lived.'

For a second she gazed at him in a haze of confusion, then the obvious burst upon her. 'You thought I was lying.' He didn't reply, and as full comprehension dawned she opened her eyes wide. 'You thought I was meeting someone.'

His grey gaze met hers and slid away. 'I—it seemed a possibility.'

She stared at him in amazement. Barely aware of its origins, she felt pain slice through her. Her lips hardly seemed able to form the words. 'But how could you, after—?'

Images crowded in on her. Their first night. All the times they'd made love, the things they'd said to each other, the tenderness, her passion for him. What had it all meant? She made a helpless, inarticulate gesture. 'So what did you think?' Her voice trembled. 'That I run from your arms to someone else's? I sleep with *you* so I must be a slut?'

He winced. 'Of course I don't think that.'

'But that must be what you think.' Tears sprang into her

eyes. The unbearable implication seeped through her brain and solidified into an ice cold certainty. There was no way he could love her, if he thought about her in such a way.

Her voice grew hoarse. 'Have you been thinking this all along? Is it because I'm a blonde? An easy screw?'

His eyes flared and he gripped her shoulders. 'Don't talk like that.'

'Why? Because that is what you think?' She shook him off. 'Or… Oh, no, no. It's because I'm a reporter.' An absurd possibility swam into her mind. 'Do you think I'm working to expose all your secrets?'

He made an impulsive gesture as if to stop her from saying the unspeakable, and the extreme suspicion was confirmed. A couple came out of the entrance, forcing her to turn aside for dignity's sake. When they were past she continued, her low voice croaky with emotion. 'You know very well I could have flagged your deal with Olivia three weeks ago. *Should* have. So how *can* you—?' She broke off, shaking her head. 'You must think I'm very calculating. Do I seem so—dishonest to you, Tom?'

At the hurt in her white face something twisted in Tom's chest. 'You don't,' he said urgently. 'Of course you don't. I've made a mistake. I know you always said you were visiting your grandmother… I don't know how I came to imagine…' He felt his blood pressure rising, and gesticulated with both hands. 'Don't look like that. You—*this*—you don't know what you—what it means to me.'

'The sex, you mean?' The wry inflection in her voice stabbed at his gut even as he tried to decipher what she intended by the words. She turned her back on him. 'Well, it's over now. Anyway, I have to go and help Gran with her meal.'

He grabbed her and turned her to face him. 'Listen,' he said, fierce in his need for reason to reign. 'You've been bloody secretive. You *know* that businesswise this is a critical time for me. I needed to know… What did you expect me to think?'

The green eyes assessing him were stern and unrelenting. 'I expected you to trust me.' The smooth arms so recently alive to his caress felt stiff and unyielding in his hands. He had no option but to release her. Then she walked back inside.

CHAPTER THIRTEEN

HE DIDN'T love her. The knowledge filled Cate with suffocating pain.

And as if that wasn't enough, Gran had recognised him.

She was forced to tell Gran some of it. The bitter irony was that while she tried to downplay the affair, since it was now irrevocably *over*, Gran seemed pleasantly enthused about Tom and kept talking him up. She said things like, 'He looks like such a nice lad.' 'He doesn't sound a bit like his father.'

When their conversation switched back to the surgery plans, Cate forced herself to concentrate, but, despite her concern, it was a struggle to keep her mind off Tom. His face kept swimming in front of her eyes.

It was over, kept replaying in her mind. Her beautiful bubble had burst. And so fast she couldn't believe it. For Gran's sake she tried to keep up a smile, but was so close to tears, she actually felt glad Gran was long-sighted.

What a fool she'd been, telling herself it didn't matter whether or not he loved her. It did. It mattered cruelly.

She didn't go back to Tom's after she and Gran said goodnight. Though most of her clothes as well as her make-up had found their way over to his place, her emotional energy had been laid too low for her to deal with him again so soon.

He phoned her several times through the evening, and she

let the phone's jangly tune play itself out. Late at night it rang again. She knew why. This was their time for love.

He wanted her.

Only it wasn't love, not on his side. In a former life she'd been through all this. As tempting as it was to accept any excuse he gave and crawl back into his bed as if she hadn't seen the stark truth, she knew she had to be strong.

She sat on the edge of her narrow bed in the boarding house, the phone vibrating in her palm while she struggled with herself. She gave in, of course, and held it to her ear, listening for his voice with painful longing. But as soon as he spoke she cut in with, 'This is no use, Tom. Please don't try to sweet-talk me. It's over.'

There was a long, pricking silence, then he said in a raw voice, 'That sounds very definite.'

Her whole body clenched. 'There's no going back. There's no changing what—what you think of me.' Her voice wobbled at the end.

She heard his fierce intake of breath. 'What I might have wondered for five minutes is *not* what I—' He broke off, then after a few turbulent moments said very quietly, 'It's true I made a stupid mistake, but it may have showed us both some uncomfortable truths. Perhaps you're right. Perhaps we both need to take stock. Realistically speaking, I'm not sure how long I can stay with a woman who so clearly feels ashamed of me.'

She gasped. 'Oh, Tom. That's not—that's in *no way* what I said. When it comes right down to it, I'm the one who—'

Her eyes swam with tears. What she wanted to say was that she was the one who loved him and had done all the giving, but the words were taboo and choked her up. Instead, she filled the gap with, 'Being with you is—*was*—a risk for me.'

'A risk!' He was silent, then said grimly, 'Let it be, then. I suppose it had to end sooner or later.'

The blood drained from her heart.

After that she turned the phone off. It wasn't that she

expected him to call again. She just knew she wouldn't be able to talk to anyone without crying. She lay down in her bed, and let devastation set in. If he'd had the slightest feeling for her, would he have accepted it was over so easily?

She thought of all the things she loved about him, the times they'd laughed, and suffered an agony of yearning so intense she could have doubled up with the pain.

After a long intense weep she tried to view the situation objectively. She'd been such a fool, deluding herself so thoroughly into her romantic dream state. The stark, unvarnished reality was, she'd allowed herself to become a rich man's mistress—not even a mistress, in fact. A short-term fling.

Face it. She'd been a handy diversion to him. A distracting interlude after the sadness of his father's death. Now it was humiliatingly clear that the tough business operator in him had never let him lose sight of who and what she was. How ironic, when she'd let go of all her reservations about him.

Not that she had been ashamed of him. The unfairness of that remark utterly mystified her. She'd explained about Gran's heart condition, hadn't she? And if he was referring to how she'd kept their affair a secret from her friends, he must have known how it would have complicated things for her at work to have it made public.

As for her being *secretive*—the accusation had hit her on the raw. She scrolled back through the days and nights to see if there'd been any justification for it. She had, of course, been to see Gran every day, and hadn't always said where she was going. And why should she have? She was a free and independent woman living in a democracy, wasn't she?

The boarding-house bed must have been made of rock ice. But the aching physical torment of not having Tom's big warm body wrapped around her, his hand cupping her breast, was nothing compared to the anguish of knowing her love for him was unrequited. She cried into her pillow like a Hunter Valley rain depression.

In the morning there was a text from him on her phone about her clothes, but she couldn't face the ruthless finality of it, and deleted it without reading it properly.

She looked like hell. The bags under her puffy eyes were only outdone by the misery lines around her mouth. She had to rely on her compact, and drops in her eyes, to make herself human enough for work. Not that it mattered. Who would see her there?

She managed to rake up a passable skirt and top, but short of buying a new wardrobe, knew she'd have to find some way of collecting her things from Tom without seeing him.

On the train to work a scenario raised its head she should never have allowed herself to contemplate. The one where, when she went proudly back for her things, he was so pleased to see her, he apologised on his knees and begged her to come back to him. In the fantasy she was stern and unforgiving, and that was when he told her he loved her.

The impossibility of this actually happening, given that he considered her to be the type of person to betray him with another man, brought more tears to her eyes. The reality was, he'd demonstrated that he wasn't a man who would beg a woman, and knowing it only made her yearn for him more.

At work, Marge gave her some sidelong glances and muttered something to herself about people who were gluttons for punishment.

It was the longest day on record. Though she didn't expect him to, not really, he didn't phone again. It was obvious what it meant. Out of sight, out of his life. On the third day she returned home in the evening to find her baggage neatly piled in the downstairs hall.

It was like a javelin through her chest. Nothing could have been more final.

When she arrived at work the next morning, she permitted herself a last legitimate reason to text him, thanking him for having her things delivered back to the Lady Musgrave. Her desk phone rang almost immediately. She picked it up with a shaking hand and heard his deep, crisp voice. He sounded controlled and unemotional.

'If you want that interview about the West-Russell merger, I can give you an hour today at eleven o'clock.'

That was all. No apologies. No attempt to suss out her feelings. She could tell by his businesslike tone exactly how he'd looked when he'd said it. Cool, serious.

Gorgeous.

She unravelled into chaos. She needed to be strong, but… Admit it. It was a chance to see him. Regardless of how he'd hurt her, she couldn't deny herself seeing him one more time. And she'd earned that interview. Despite what he'd suspected she was capable of, she'd kept her end of the bargain.

In accordance with *Clarion* rules, she was supposed to inform Harry of the interview offer. That faced her with a dilemma. Harry would expect her to take a photographer with her. If she did that there'd be no opportunity for any personal exchange, but if she went alone, Tom would assume she had expectations. Hopes, even. And face it—alone, could she trust herself to maintain her dignity?

In the end, she did mention it to Harry, who immediately assigned Mike to go with her. She could have cringed at the surprised flicker of respect in Harry's eyes. If only he knew how far her personal feelings had overridden her professional responsibilities.

By the time she found Mike resting his bones against a wall at their rendezvous on the ground floor of the Russell building, her insides were in turmoil. What could she and Tom possibly say to each other? Against all reason, the certainty— *hope*—grew in her mind that he was using this interview as an opportunity to get her back.

His phone call had set the tone for how she must behave. Cool, professional and unemotional. Dignified. Dispassionate. She retied the ribbon securing her hair in her nape and smoothed her slim, sand-coloured skirt and crisp white shirt.

Riding up in the glass-walled lift with Mike, she caught brief glimpses of various newsrooms in the throes of churning out cheap Russell trash, but felt too emotional to bother ridiculing them.

A sleek receptionist on the fiftieth floor invited them to be seated outside Tom's office. Mike deposited his equipment, then stretched out on a couch and shut his eyes, while Cate paced about, inspecting the artworks with a nervous, thudding heart. For a cowardly moment she wasn't sure she would cope. Her legs felt strangely reluctant to hold her up. She was staring blindly at a drawing of some foreign skyscraper that was shaped like a sail, and had walls consisting entirely of solar panels, when the door opened.

Tom strode out, looking sophisticated and authoritative in his dark suit. Her heart thundered so painfully she could scarcely breathe.

Immediately his grey gaze trapped hers for spark-showering seconds. The heavy sexual current pulsed between them, barely distinguishable from anguish. His glance flicked sharply to Mike, caught in the act of hauling himself lazily to his feet, and his expression hardened.

With his sensuous mouth firmly compressed, he forced her into a brief, disturbing handshake. As his lean, hard palm connected with hers the electric desire sizzled through her veins. How could bodies be so treacherous? She read his knowledge of her yearning in his fierce gaze. He still wanted her, she could sense it.

Overcoming his apparent annoyance at her having brought a companion, he turned his attention to Mike. 'Don't tell me,' he said, extending his hand with polished courtesy. 'Mike.'

The smile in his eyes as he guessed the photographer's identity from her description was an added assault to the sore spot in her heart. He'd looked at her sometimes with just that gleam. How could he feel amusement *now*?

In ignorance of her pain and regret, he ushered them both inside, smoothly enquiring of Mike how he preferred to work.

Mike suggested they start the interview, and he'd take his shots when they'd warmed up a little and relaxed. As *if*.

Tom showed them to a leather lounge suite, and said, further destabilising Cate's shaky façade, 'How's your grandmother?'

She was taken aback. Did he have any idea how inflammatory that question was? Speechless at first, she dredged up a few dry, incoherent words, then, with a sense of unreality, started through the motions of her profession.

She sat opposite Tom in an armchair, and took out her notebook and cassette. Thoughts whirred round and round in her head. How could they have come to this? A few days ago they'd been lovers. It seemed so painful and absurd not to be able to touch him, or even look at him properly.

Screamingly conscious of the vibrations in the charged air, she felt his glance raze her face and hands and legs. If only they could bury the sword that lay between them. If the disaster had never happened...

If *only* he hadn't revealed his true colours...

But it was no use grieving. She had a job to do.

'Do you mind?' she said, placing her recorder on the coffee table.

'Please. Go ahead.' She felt rather than saw the smooth gesture of his lean hand.

His PA brought coffee in, though Mike declined, preferring to prowl around to get the feel of the room. While the coffee was poured Tom maintained an easy flow of conversation. As if he'd never held her in his arms, and they'd never been lovers.

He handed her some coffee, careful not to touch her.

He was playing it straight, she realised with a sinking heart. The interview was for real. He was just fulfilling their bargain. She hardly knew what she said, she felt so miserably unable to come to terms with the new status quo. But even if it had been attainable, the old status quo could never work again. Not now she knew the truth.

At last he paused to look mockingly at her, and it was time to begin.

She cleared her croaky throat. 'How does it feel, Mr Russell, to be among the hundred wealthiest people in the world?'

'I'm not among them,' he said. 'I'm not even among the thousand wealthiest. Or the ten thousand wealthiest. Not at the moment, that is.'

As shock reverberated around the walls she noticed Mike's gaze whip round, and was aware of him lifting his video camera onto his shoulder for an online grab.

She stared at Tom in puzzled disbelief. 'But—your inheritance.'

'What very few people know, Cate— May I call you Cate?' he enquired, tearing her heart out '—is that before his death my father made over most of his fortune to the Developing World Foundation. You've heard of that?'

If he'd hit her with a stun gun she couldn't have been more thoroughly knocked out. Of course she'd heard of it. Everyone knew of the trust set up by the richest man in the world. In the name of morality, and perhaps the chance to make it through the pearly gates, other billionaires were now scrambling to join him on the nobility bandwagon.

But Marcus Russell?

The information was startling, to say the least. It certainly explained why Tom's company had needed a merger. While her brain fast-tracked to slot the news in with all the events she'd witnessed since the conversation in the cathedral, Tom said, 'It will come as a surprise to the *Clarion*'s readers, no doubt, that my father had a conscience.'

'I apologised to you about that,' she said hotly, flushing.

'Yes, you did.' His sensual gaze rested on her face. 'And very stirringly. I can't recall a more heartfelt apology.'

It was cruel of him to bring that up. A potent image of the

first night they'd made love rose before her. Tears pricked her eyes and she had to lower her glance. But, remembering Mike, she scrambled to steer the subject away from the danger zone.

'Is this why you're selling all your houses?'

He hesitated. 'Not altogether. And I'm only selling the ones I feel a need to break with.'

'Oh.' She swallowed. 'And does that include the Château Bleu?'

'I think so. I'm finding it very large.'

She cast him a veiled glance. Was he implying that it felt lonely? Without her?

'Anyway,' she said huskily, 'now that you have—control of—Russell Inc, what are your plans for the future? I mean, your *company's* future? Not your—personal future, of course.'

'Of course. What possible interest could Cate Summerfield have in my personal future?'

Stung by the injustice, she leaned forward. 'Look, I wasn't the one who ruined things. I wasn't the one who didn't trust *you.*'

The response shot back like a bullet. 'Did you trust me, though? It seems pretty clear to me you didn't trust me to measure up in your grandmother's eyes.'

'Oh,' she gasped. 'That wasn't it at *all*. I told you. You know I told you about Gran's heart. She's very fragile. She went through a distressing incident a while back and it caused her to have a heart attack that was very nearly fatal. And that was *all my fault*. I couldn't possibly risk that happening again.' Suddenly she noticed the camera directed straight at her and Mike's fascinated gaze. 'Cut that out, Mike,' she screeched in dismay. 'I'm not part of this story.'

Tom looked amused and she turned sharply to him. 'If you wouldn't mind just keeping to the questions.' There was no concealing the raw emotion in her voice.

He lowered his black lashes. To hide his satisfaction, she was willing to bet. Now that he'd drawn blood. After a few smouldering seconds he spoke again.

'In answer to your question, I'm downsizing Russell Inc. Instead of eighteen diverse companies it will now simply be two. One—which controls my tabloid and magazine holdings—is in the process of merging with the West Corporation as we speak. The other will require my full and personal attention for some time. I want to establish a quality national daily to compete with papers like the *Clarion*. You'll find the details in here.' He took up some papers from the coffee table and handed them across. 'I intend to raid your market, so you people had better look to your laurels.' He turned towards Mike. 'Thanks mate. That'll be all.'

Mike looked a little taken aback, but didn't argue. He packed up his equipment, thanked Tom with a brief hand-shake, and, shooting her a quizzical glance, left.

The room fell silent. She could feel Tom's eyes on her as she finished making her notes, and slotted her notebook and cassette back into her bag. At the edge of her vision she could see his expensive trouser leg and polished leather shoe. She didn't know why it should cut her up, but it did, that today he'd remembered his socks.

'Well,' she mumbled, rising jerkily to her feet, 'thanks for the interview. I guess we're square now.'

He stood up as well. 'I'm sorry I hurt you on Sunday. You had every reason to be angry.'

'No doubt you felt driven by the need to protect your business interests.'

The glint in his eyes told her he'd felt the barb. She waited, but he made no answering shot. Why didn't he defend himself? If he wanted her in the slightest degree, wouldn't he try to persuade her now with some reason she could gra-ciously accept? She realised with desperation that now the old status quo was the most desirable situation she could ever have offered to her in her life.

She made a reluctant move towards the door. He made no effort to detain her and she felt a surge of panic. This would be the last time they'd ever meet. Was there nothing worth salvaging?

He walked with her, and as he opened the door she hesitated, then turned to face him. Her heart nearly failed her at the risk she was taking, but, ignoring the warning signs, she screwed up her courage to say haltingly, 'I had thought, Tom—I'd *hoped*, that is—that you might—that we could—work something out. No—no strings attached, of course.'

As soon as the words were out fear nearly crushed her lungs. Her defenceless heart lay before him, naked and quivering on the chopping block.

His eyes veiled. 'Something?'

An excruciated blush rose at her ankles and flooded right through to her scalp, then just as quickly drained and left her cold.

As though seeing how mortified she felt, he took her arms in a light, firm grip and said gravely, 'Sweetheart, I've been in the kind of relationship before where we weren't open and straight with each other. The rot set in so fast then, I'm not sure I'll ever be up for that again.'

It took a while for the rejection to filter through. Her pain was so severe, she knew her breezy, careless smile must have looked more like the fixed grin of a death's head, but she kept it nailed in place and gasped in a constricted voice, 'Oh. Oh, well, then. No worries. So long, then. I—I'd better get back to the newsroom.'

Before he could release her she wrenched herself from his grasp and walked quickly to the lifts, her mind and body numb. Mike was waiting downstairs. She just shoved past him and said, 'Shut up, Mike,' then broke into a run. Her agonised grin was still frozen to her face when she arrived back at work.

She sat at her desk and wrote her big scoop like a robot. After she'd filed she took a hard copy into Harry, laid it before him on his desk and in a dull, toneless voice confessed the gory details of her massive conflict of interest. Predictably, he hit the roof, but when his incredulous stream of curses stopped raining down on her head, she said, 'All right. I'm sorry. Take it or leave it. It's your call.'

She knew what they'd do in the end. It was too fabulous a story to kill. It would go to print, but she felt no victory. Instead, her heart was a well of tears.

At Autumn Leaves, there'd been more news. In keeping with the flow of the day so far, her grandmother's operation had been postponed for another three months due to a shortage in hospital staff. Gran acted as though it were just a minor hitch, and Cate held her weakened hand and tried to think of upbeat things to say.

She stayed with her as long as she possibly could while still able to conceal the massive lump in her throat. Then after they'd said goodnight, she dragged herself home, climbed the stairs to her bed without speaking to anyone, and crawled under the duvet like a bleeding animal.

CHAPTER FOURTEEN

A COMMOTION of voices in the hall outside Cate's door brought her head up from her pillow. Through the haze of tears she blinked blearily at her clock radio and saw that it was after eight. Strangely, she could hear male voices. She reached for her bedside lamp, then sprang up in alarm. There was one male voice in particular. A voice she knew well. At almost the same instant a knock came on her door. A firm, decisive knock.

Squinting to accustom herself to the lamplight, she sat staring at the door, the duvet bunched to her chest. How could Tom be here?

'Cate.' He knocked again. 'Cate, are you in there?'

Someone must have told him he wasn't allowed on her floor because she heard him snap, 'Look, get lost mate.' Before her mesmerised gaze the door opened a crack, then a few inches further, and Tom put his head around. 'Can I come in?'

Shock outweighed the horror of being caught red-eyed and blotchy. It was just as well, because without waiting for an invitation, Tom walked in and closed the door behind him. He strolled right over to her bed and sat down on it. She could see how abject she must have looked by the dismay and concern he was rapidly trying to conceal from her.

'Are you all right?' His voice had deepened further, as if he were severely shaken.

It was too late to dive under the covers or reach for a paper bag to slip over her head, so she was forced to brazen it out. Whatever he was here for, whether it was to rebuke her, or add something he'd forgotten to his merger story, she was too emotionally drained to protest or even put on a façade. So she just nodded.

His face was strained and taut. 'How—how is she?'

Cate stared at him, bemusement competing with other powerful emotions. 'Gran, you mean?' Her voice sounded as croaky as a hermit's.

'Yes, Gran. Look, I wanted to tell you today. There was so much I wanted to say to you, but things got way out of control.' He gave a painful grimace and her heart panged with the remembrance. He took her hands and held them firmly, compelling her with his urgent gaze. 'I think we should get her out of that place. I did a fair bit of research into those facilities when Dad was sick, and… Look, sweetheart, I know a good man—a top heart man. He's prepared to see her just as soon as she gives him the nod. He attends an excellent little private hospital at Rose Bay. I'll take you down there if you like and you can see what you think of it.' He spoke persuasively, as if he expected a wall of resistance. 'It's not far. And then we can talk about where she'd prefer to recuperate. She might want to live with us.'

'Oh.' It was all she could think of to say. What was going on here? Was she still in with a chance with Tom Russell? A stunned, fearful joy bobbed on her sea of despair and lifted its tiny face to the sun. 'Why—why…I mean…Why do you…? You know I can't afford…'

Tom Russell put his finger over her lips and shook his head. He said, as if the answer were obvious, 'She's your *grandmother*.'

His eyes were fierce and tender and sincere, like the night he'd said that he'd adore her for ever. She felt such a burst of love for him. In that moment she knew she could never love anyone as much as she loved him. Not if she lived to be a thousand.

Right on cue, at perhaps the most crucial moment of her life to date, the one where it was most critical for her to be in control of her faculties, hot tears started streaming from her eyes like a lava flow from a subterranean river.

Tom Russell put his arms around her and kissed her face and hair. Sobbing, she clung to him as if she were a drowning woman. He crawled into the narrow bed beside her, lay her down with him and held her against his hard body. He stroked her tenderly and she could feel his big, strong heart pounding against hers through the thin fabrics of her blouse and his tee shirt. It was so comforting. And such a blissful relief. For once she let another human being besides Gran soothe her as if she were a child.

When the worst of the flood had abated he reached over to her bedside table for a handful of tissues so she could mop up. She sat up and did her best to repair the damage.

'I'm so sorry,' she said when she could, her voice as wobbly as her knees. 'I don't usually dissolve like that. I must look awful.'

'You could never look awful.' His voice was thick and his eyes shone with an earnest sincerity. 'You're the most beautiful woman I've ever seen.'

What was wrong with him? Was he short-sighted? No other man in the world could look at her as she was now and think she was beautiful.

'I'm not usually a weeper,' she persevered explaining, disregarding his strange opinions while she blew her nose. 'It's just that Gran's news hasn't been very good lately. And I've been on my own this week.' Her voice made another dangerous wobble.

He winced and looked guilt-stricken. 'I know. That was—bloody criminal. None of it should have happened. It was me. I—' He shut his eyes for an instant. She could see his Adam's apple working in his strong bronzed throat. 'I shouldn't have followed you, I knew that. You see I felt... When I saw you talking to that guy...'

'Steve?'

His handsome jaw hardened slightly. 'Him, yes. I have to admit I was—jealous. I saw how he looked at you that night and I thought—God knows what I thought. And oh, God…I do hope—' Anxiety clouded his gaze. 'It's been worrying me, Cate. Did I—did I put your grandmother's health in jeopardy when I blundered in there the other day?'

She flushed. 'No. No, you didn't at all, in fact. I over-reacted. I got such a shock, seeing you there. You see, a similar thing happened—well, not similar, not at all…in *no way* the same—once before. When I was engaged to Steve.' She cast him an apologetic glance. 'Gran's heart condition had just been diagnosed and she was in hospital for tests. I think Steve felt resentful for all the time I was spending with her, because he said something pretty hurtful while we were visiting Gran. And you know me. I flared up like a firecracker, and *I* said things, and *he* said things…then poor Gran just—just…'

She choked up and the tears started again. Would there ever be any end to them?

But far from being disgusted or impatient, Tom Russell wound his arms around her and rocked her, murmuring soothing things like, 'Shh, shh' and, 'There, there, my darling, it wasn't your fault' until the floodgates clanged shut once more. Being called 'my darling' helped a lot, to tell the truth.

When she'd recovered a bit of composure, Tom leaned back against the headboard and said, 'Was that why your engagement broke?'

She shrugged. 'Oh, that was the deciding moment. But there were other things, too. You know, we didn't have much in common. You know how I feel about football, and poor Steve wouldn't know what a symphony orchestra was if it ambushed him. And he didn't think I could ever be a good reporter.' She gazed mistily at him. 'I can't believe that you of all people would think you had any reason to be jealous. Of *anyone.*'

He looked embarrassed, then lowered his gaze in shame.

'I was such an idiot to be suspicious of you. You've been nothing but honest. You're truly the most sincere and beautiful girl I ever knew. You don't know—you'll never know how you—light up my soul.'

She blushed at the compliment. It was true her passion for him was sincere, but she was beginning to think he had an inflated idea of her. Still, she didn't want to stop him from saying more fantastic things she could store up for future reference to dwell on in bed on some rainy afternoon. He was gazing at her in a way that made her insides flutter with a tremulous, joyful hope, and she held her breath, on a tingling edge for what he might say next.

His stunning grey eyes bathed her in their warm, earnest glow. 'I'll try to explain. Before I met you I might have been going through some sort of a—a negative period. I think perhaps it affected my judgement about—you know, trusting people. Then when I found you, right from that first night…'

'That fabulous night,' she whispered.

'That fabulous night,' he echoed, giving her a swift, fierce kiss, 'Since that night, my precious girl, everything in my life feels—different. The last thing I intended was to mess it all up. I was such a dim-witted fool. And then today didn't go as planned.'

'No. But at least we're talking again,' she said hopefully.

'Exactly.' He heaved a long sigh. 'Thank God. What we said today—you know, about no strings attached… What I wanted to tell you, and made a bloody mess of…' He broke off to drag a hand though his hair. 'Well, I'm not really the no-strings-attached kind of guy.'

Her heart skidded to a crazy halt. 'Aren't you?' she breathed.

'No.' He gazed silently at her for such a long time, she began to think he'd said all he was going to say. Then he added quietly, 'Well, you know, Cate, I'm in love with you.'

She knew she should say something, but the power of speech was thrilled out of her.

He looked searchingly at her, and his deep voice grew gruff and gravelly with emotion. 'I love you so—*intensely*, I was hoping you felt the same way. It *feels* as if you must.' He was breathing jerkily, as if the words were being wrenched from a place deeper than the place where the Ferrari dwelled. 'And if you could…if you *do*—if we love each other, I think we should agree to some strings.' For an instant uncertainty clouded his eyes. 'That's if you want that. I know it's sudden. But it's right. For me, anyway. What do you think? Do you…?'

She stared at him. Tears sprang into her eyes while her heart sang like a joyous choir of magpies. Then she put her arms around Tom Russell and kissed him with all the tenderness and passionate joy in her heart. 'Yes, yes, Tom, I do love you. I love you extremely.'

He wiped his brow and grinned. 'Whew. Thank God for that. Then do you think you could risk marrying me?'

She laughed with the overflow of emotion. 'You bet I'll risk it, lover. I will. Oh, I certainly will.'

There wasn't much room in the single bed. Tom Russell stretched out beside her, grazing her temple with his bristly jaw while they planned the ring, a whole programme of wedding music and—provided Gran was safely out of the woods—a honeymoon in Tuscany.

It wasn't long, though, before she heard the thud of his shoes hitting the floor. In truth, earlier, when she'd been sobbing into his tee shirt, she'd had reason to suspect that something like this might happen.

'There are rules at the Lady Musgrave,' she whispered when his sinful intentions became clear.

'Shh. Shh.'

HARLEQUIN *Presents*

Undressed
BY THE BOSS

From sensible suits…into satin sheets!

Stranded in a Nevada hotel, Kate throws herself
on the mercy of hotelier Zack Boudreaux.
In exchange for a job and a way home, he'll
make her his very personal assistant….

THE TYCOON'S VERY PERSONAL ASSISTANT
by Heidi Rice
Book # 2761

Available in September:

If you love stories about a gorgeous boss, look out for:

BUSINESS IN THE BEDROOM
by Anne Oliver
Book # 2770

Available next month in Harlequin Presents.

HP12761

REQUEST YOUR
FREE BOOKS!

HARLEQUIN *Presents*®

2 FREE NOVELS
PLUS 2
FREE GIFTS!

PASSION
GUARANTEED
SEDUCTION

YES! Please send me 2 FREE Harlequin Presents® novels and my 2 FREE gifts (gifts are worth about $10). After receiving them, if I don't wish to receive any more books, I can return the shipping statement marked "cancel". If I don't cancel, I will receive 6 brand-new novels every month and be billed just $4.05 per book in the U.S. or $4.74 per book in Canada, plus 25¢ shipping and handling per book and applicable taxes, if any*. That's a savings of close to 15% off the cover price! I understand that accepting the 2 free books and gifts places me under no obligation to buy anything. I can always return a shipment and cancel at any time. Even if I never buy another book, the two free books and gifts are mine to keep forever.

106 HDN ERRW   306 HDN ERRL

Name	(PLEASE PRINT)	
Address		Apt. #
City	State/Prov.	Zip/Postal Code

Signature (if under 18, a parent or guardian must sign)

Mail to the **Harlequin Reader Service:**
IN U.S.A.: P.O. Box 1867, Buffalo, NY 14240-1867
IN CANADA: P.O. Box 609, Fort Erie, Ontario L2A 5X3

Not valid to current subscribers of Harlequin Presents books.

Want to try two free books from another line?
Call 1-800-873-8635 or visit www.morefreebooks.com.

* Terms and prices subject to change without notice. N.Y. residents add applicable sales tax. Canadian residents will be charged applicable provincial taxes and GST. Offer not valid in Quebec. This offer is limited to one order per household. All orders subject to approval. Credit or debit balances in a customer's account(s) may be offset by any other outstanding balance owed by or to the customer. Please allow 4 to 6 weeks for delivery. Offer available while quantities last.

Your Privacy: Harlequin Books is committed to protecting your privacy. Our Privacy Policy is available online at www.eHarlequin.com or upon request from the Reader Service. From time to time we make our lists of customers available to reputable third parties who may have a product or service of interest to you. If you would prefer we not share your name and address, please check here. ☐

HP08R

▼ Silhouette®

SPECIAL EDITION™

NEW YORK TIMES BESTSELLING AUTHOR

DIANA PALMER

A brand-new Long, Tall Texans novel

HEART OF STONE

Feeling unwanted and unloved, Keely returns to Jacobsville and to Boone Sinclair, a rancher troubled by his own past. Boone has always seemed reserved, but now Keely discovers a sensuality with him that quickly turns to love. Can they each see past their own scars to let love in?

*Available September 2008
wherever you buy books.*

EXTRA

AN INNOCENT IN HIS BED

He's a man who takes whatever he
pleases—even if it means bedding
an inexperienced young woman....

With his intense good looks, commanding presence
and unquestionable power, he'll carefully charm her
and entice her into his bed, where he'll teach her
the ways of love—by giving her the most amazingly
sensual night of her life!

**Don't miss any of the exciting stories
in September:**

#21 THE CATTLE BARON'S VIRGIN WIFE
by LINDSAY ARMSTRONG

**#22 THE GREEK TYCOON'S
INNOCENT MISTRESS**
by KATHRYN ROSS

#23 PREGNANT BY THE ITALIAN COUNT
by CHRISTINA HOLLIS

#24 ANGELO'S CAPTIVE VIRGIN
by INDIA GREY